USA *TODAY* BESTSELLING AUTHOR
Dale Mayer

SEALS OF HONOR
Lachlan

BOOK-28

LACHLAN: SEALS OF HONOR, BOOK 28
Dale Mayer
Valley Publishing

ISBN-13: 978-1-773365-72-5
Print Edition

Books in This Series:

About This Book

Lachlan is delighted to be picked by Tesla to help her friend out in Germany on a sensitive joint operation. Yet, when he finds out what's involved, he's shocked and intrigued. He's not so overjoyed at the several references to how this "friend" would be perfect for him.

Leah is relatively new to her job as a military analyst based in Germany. When her department is asked to help in a joint task force, she's afraid she's in over her head. She's worked with several of these people before, but this case is an international banking scandal, which everyone is anxious to keep out of the media. But that's pretty hard to do when the kidnapped victims survive, and a loved one doesn't.

As the bodies pile up, Lachlan realizes this is more about keeping Leah safe and less about helping Tesla out. It doesn't take long for him to agree, and she becomes his priority too.

Sign up to be notified of all Dale's releases here!
https://smarturl.it/DaleNews

COMPLIMENTARY DOWNLOAD

DOWNLOAD a *__complimentary__* copy of TUESDAY'S CHILD? Just tell me where to send it!

http://dalemayer.com/starterlibrarytc/

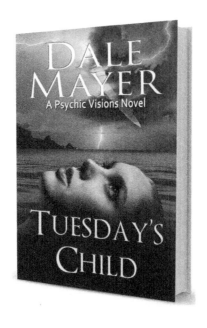

PROLOGUE

L ACHLAN MACGAVIN WALKED into the huge conference
room. He'd been with Mason's team for a few months
now and when Mason had called, Lachlan had stepped up.
One thing that Mason had that Lachlan would like to have
in his own future was the respect of everybody he knew
around him. As he walked into the empty schoolroom setup,
he frowned to see Mason sitting there, with a stack of papers
in front of him. "Hell of a place for a meeting."

Mason looked up. "Yeah, we've got computer training
coming up. I do get tired of it, but it's important to stay on
top of the new techniques."

"Absolutely." Lachlan sat down beside Mason. "You
called me in, so what's up?"

Mason laughed. "I always liked that about you. A
straight shooter all the way."

"Don't really have time for games," Lachlan replied in a
mild voice.

"Nope, I hear you there. I've got somebody telling me
that you're quite the electronics guy."

"Well, I am," Lachlan agreed, "but I don't think I've got
anything on Tesla."

"She's in a world unto herself. But she's the one who
told me that you were really good."

Lachlan found himself smiling at that. "Praise from her

is high praise, indeed. Tell her thanks."

"Not an issue," Mason stated. "So I was thinking I'd get you in here, while we do some other training."

"What are you doing training on?" he asked.

"Security, but more for our own offices."

Lachlan winced at that.

"Not exactly your thing, I know," Mason noted, "but we have an interesting case that we're tracking right now. We've got a hacker out of England, hitting banks in Europe."

"What's that got to do with us?"

"It's a joint task force," he explained, "with Germany. Because they suspect it originated from a joint team of hackers in England and Germany. We've been asked to send in specialists to help, if we have anybody."

"Is Tesla going?"

"She'd love to," he replied, "but no."

"So?"

"The idea is that you would work with her. You would be her field person over there, while she works from here."

Lachlan looked at him in surprise. "Wow. Is this …?" And he stopped, a little confused.

Mason looked over at him and smiled. "Basically Tesla would like you on the team. She'd like you to be her eyes and ears."

"I'd be honored," he stated. "I'm just not sure what capacity this would be in."

"You'd be heading over with two of our men."

"Two?"

"Markus and potentially Axel."

"And the three of us will do what?"

"Sort out exactly what's going on."

"And we're expecting it to be out of Germany, not England?"

"We do have a few feelers out in Germany. MI6 will be there, and you'll coordinate with Jonas."

At that, Lachlan winced.

Mason grinned. "Everybody loves Jonas."

"Sure, but Jonas doesn't love any of us," he murmured.

"See? That makes you so perfect for this. You already understand the lay of the land."

"And who are we coordinating with in Germany?" Lachlan asked.

"Her name is Leah," he responded. "She's a friend of Tesla. She's in a similar position to Tesla's here, but she's green and new to the job. New to the post. She's set up for a six-month stint there in Germany. Tesla wants to make sure Leah has the help she needs, and you're to keep Tesla in the loop. And me."

"Okay, that sounds decent."

"Yep." Then Mason grinned.

"What's that grin for?" Lachlan asked, staring at him.

"Nothing. Just that Tesla is of the opinion that you two would be a great pair."

Lachlan's heart sank, and he glared at Mason. "Oh no, not happening. None of that."

"None of what?" Mason asked.

"No matchmaking."

"Not me." Mason raised his hands, with an innocent look.

"No, not at all," Lachlan repeated. "No matchmaking."

"If it's not to be"—he shrugged—"I presume you wouldn't have anything to do with Leah."

"What does that mean?"

"If you don't find her attractive and if there isn't any

chemistry, then you have nothing to worry about."

Lachlan stared at his friend suspiciously. "That sounds dubiously like a sidestep."

Mason laughed. "This training is about to start." He straightened up his stack of papers, as the door opened, and more guys sauntered in. "Is that a yes or a no?"

"It's a hell yes," Lachlan replied immediately. "When do I leave?"

Mason looked at him with a smile. "Yesterday."

He rolled his eyes and asked, "Seriously?"

"You leave in less than three hours. So get your gear, and I'll set it up."

"On it." As Lachlan walked to the door, he watched as everybody else filed in for the computer upgrade session. Then he looked over at Mason, who was watching him. Lachlan shook his head at him. "No matchmaking." He pointed his finger for emphasis.

Mason gave him a thumbs-up and a big grin.

And Lachlan knew he was already halfway lost.

The only way to prove Mason wrong was to get there, to find out Lachlan had absolutely nothing to worry about, and to carry on.

Tesla had asked for him, huh? For that, he was pretty damn happy. He loved working with her, and she was one smart cookie. If there was anything or anyone he wouldn't mind learning under, it would be her. Smiling and whistling, he headed home to get ready to go.

CHAPTER 1

Germany

LACHLAN MACGAVIN HELD out his ID as he entered the US Army Garrison Stuttgart—or USAG Stuttgart for short. He hadn't really expected to end up here, but he was being rerouted here for the moment. As long as he got wherever he needed to go, the logistics didn't really matter, not as far as he was concerned. He reminded himself that he was here for Tesla's and Leah's sake and for the assistance that potentially could be required by Markus. Axel was apparently already here.

Lost in thought, Lachlan heard a shout and looked over to see the man himself walking toward him. Smiling, Lachlan headed that way, reaching out to shake hands.

"There you are," Axel greeted Lachlan with a big grin. "What did you guys do? Take the long way around?"

"Felt like it," Lachlan replied, feeling the weight of the international travel he had endured. "But we're here now."

"Grab your bags, and let's go."

"Are we staying here?" Lachlan asked, looking around in surprise.

"We're meeting up near here, but we have places to go and things to do," Axel replied. "Or make that people to see. Another bank CEO has been killed."

"What the hell is going on?" Lachlan asked. "Fill me in,

man."

"We've got a unique hacker situation, focusing on banks, but the hackers aren't holding data hostage but real people, yet with a twist. We've got the bad guys kidnapping someone associated with a bank, like a manager or somebody in the actual bank building, but, when the bank fails to make the ransom payout," he added in a low voice, "instead of killing the hostage, the bad guys go after their CEO. Presumably because the CEOs are the ones saying no to the ransom payouts. And, just as we made the CEO connection in those previous cases in England, now the bad guys are expanding into Germany."

He relayed as much as he could as they moved through the airport. "Remember that ransomware pipeline fiasco a few years back, where the company paid five million to the hackers to get back into their own website? Well, hacker prices have gone way up, and I think these hackers are asking for twenty-seven million for this latest one. The bank said no from the start and told the kidnappers that the bank doesn't do hostage negotiations and that they won't pay the ransom—even though they shut down the whole banking system for a couple days. Almost immediately the CEO related to that bank turned up dead. Shot in the back of the head. No witnesses. No nothing."

"Of course not. Was the kidnap victim taken from home? What do we know?"

"We don't know a hell of a lot," Axel replied in frustration. "That is where we think the hacker part comes into play. This latest dead CEO was in Germany."

"Oh, great," Lachlan muttered. "So, like Mason told me, I presume Jonas is coming then."

At that, Axel looked over at him with half a grin. "Oh,

so he's your favorite too, *huh*?" They heard a commotion not too far ahead, and there Jonas was, the one who got along with everyone. Not.

"Come on. It's not like you're all my favorite people either," Jonas snapped, his thick British accent hard to ignore.

Lachlan looked over at Jonas. "Hey, buddy. Nice to see you."

Jonas rolled his eyes. "You know what? It would be nicer if we didn't meet quite so often." He nodded to the group at large. "You guys just bring shit whenever you came over to England."

"Hey, it's not us all the time," Axel argued.

"Are you sure about that? Because it seems like it is."

"Maybe you're talking about Levi's group or Badger's."

"I am darn certain that it's all of you." Jonas raised both hands. "Sometimes I think the entire country gets overrun by your supposed goodwill police."

"Hey, we don't have to be here on goodwill," Markus added, joining the group, with a nod in greeting to Axel and Lachlan, "but it generally does get us a better footing with the locals."

"You have such a good relationship with my people," Jonas pointed out in a mocking tone.

With a dangerous grin, Markus slugged him on the shoulder. "I know you love us."

Lachlan shook his head, smirking at the male bonding going on around him.

"God, help me," Jonas replied, "I'll admit that *sometimes* I like the work you guys do. I enjoy it in the moment, but I don't enjoy the mess you leave for me to clean up?"

"You do just fine," Markus stated, with a chuckle. "I know our supposed *mess* is not that bad."

"It's not that good either," Jonas muttered. "And you do know that it would be nice if you didn't destroy Germany either, while you're here."

"We may not be in Germany for long, and maybe we'll resettle over in England," Markus teased, practically beaming, his eyebrows raised at Jonas.

"Personally I'm okay with working and living in England. At least for the moment." Axel added, "It may very well be Germany or France with these hacker types. Who cares?"

"I suspect we'll end up in England fairly quickly." Jonas frowned, as Markus and these guys enjoyed mocking MI6. "However, our present meetup is here."

They all looked over at the incoming woman, a tall, graceful, and willowy blonde. Her hair was held back in a clip, but it still fell below her waist. Just the fact that she had hair that long was amazing, considering the time it must take to care for it. She was dressed in business attire. She wore it all very well.

Lachlan reached out a hand. "I'm Lachlan MacGavin."

"I know who you are," she stated immediately. Then she smiled. "Tesla sent me photos. I'm Leah Ketridge."

He looked at her in surprise. "Too bad she didn't do the same for me," he noted cheerfully.

"Not needed. I would be the one to pick up you guys, so you'd have met me soon enough." At that, she turned and shook hands with the rest of them.

"I still don't quite understand why we're all here," Lachlan admitted.

"No, I know," she replied. "Much of it will involve doing run-around work, *boots on the ground* stuff, instead of actual computer work."

"I hope it won't be too much legwork. The more computer work, the better," Lachlan noted, his eyes twinkling. "You'll be Tesla's eyes and ears, I understand, sending her impressions and other information."

He nodded. "That's for all of us to share, right?"

"Yes, and you'll all be learning about our computer software," she murmured. "But, with this latest murder, things have gotten serious and are a hell of a lot more complicated than I anticipated. We've noted an MO. So much of the training will be pushed back."

"Right," Lachlan agreed. "I'm not exactly sure what that'll mean for us."

"It means that I don't really have time for teaching and delegation. I need information, and I need it fast. So you and your team will be helping with that."

"And you need that information from us? What about MI6? Are they not capable?" Lachlan pointed to Jonas, who sneered back at him.

Markus and Axel both shared their views, uncensored, and Lachlan stood rooted there, a smirk on his face.

Leah turned to Jonas, her own lips twitching. "I won't get into an argument there. I have worked with Jonas and his agents a couple times now." She reached out and patted his hand. "Nice to see you again, by the way."

He nodded and in a quiet voice added, "I just wish it was under better circumstances."

"Me too," she agreed. "Me too." She turned back and looked at the group of men in front of her, motioning to them all. "Too much to do and too little time. You will all have to pick up and dig in. Come on. Let's go." She turned and led the way through the building and outside. Lachlan looked over at Markus, who frowned as he followed the group. "Problems?" Lachlan asked Markus quietly.

"Not so much a problem," Markus admitted, "but this scenario means that we'll end up in the way of law enforcement." He sighed. "I was hoping to work behind the scenes. I was also looking forward to the specialized computer training."

"And that you will still get," Leah replied, overhearing their quiet conversation. "We might have to get you to stay for a few days afterward."

He nodded. "Understood. This comes first."

"It has to," she murmured. "This is the third one that we know of, two in England and now this one in Germany. We can't have this happening anymore."

"What do we know so far?" Lachlan asked. "I'm interested in the fact that they're not killing the person they are kidnapping." Lachlan was the new guy on the team, and the others let him ask the questions, so he could be brought up to speed. Plus it was no hardship for Lachlan to get his answers from a beautiful and smart woman.

"No, apparently the kidnapping appears to be a decoy," she replied, looking away. "The frustrating part is that we don't know what banks they're targeting. It appears random at the moment. We have little to nothing to go on. Hence the call for all hands on deck."

"Which is an interesting strategy, if you think about it," Lachlan murmured, "and certainly not a bad one." She looked at him, and he just shrugged. "Consider it from the hackers' perspective. All attention is focused on whoever they've kidnapped. They keep the hostage as a backup, and yet, in the meantime, they are busy working their own agenda, all behind the curtain. It's a game-theory scenario. Plain and simple."

"I get that, but I don't understand the logic behind it.

Well, the logic I do, but the purpose of the action eludes me," she murmured.

"I'm not sure there is any, other than to throw us off and to make us feel like we don't know what's going on," Lachlan suggested. "Sometimes that's all it is—divide and conquer. Throw in false leads to muddy the tracks."

"Unfortunately," Jonas added, "that's quite possible. But it doesn't help at all when it comes to finding out who's doing this. Has anybody claimed credit so far?" he asked Leah curiously.

She looked over at him and nodded. "Yes. We do have a group here who has claimed credit for the kidnapping and for the hacking. It is a big-ass black-hat group that I'm sure you've probably heard of."

He nodded as he heard the acronym. "But that group has never killed before."

"No, never, so we're not sure whether it's actually them or not."

"That would sure be a twist," Jonas noted, with a whistle. "Since, like I said, we've never known them to get involved with a killing. That way it keeps them out of that level of police scrutiny."

"Which is also BS, when you think about it," Markus stated. "I mean, they are doing the hacking, finding all this personal data on all these bank employees and the board members on up to the CEO. That information alone could be sold internationally for some big bucks, and just that thought could frighten a lot of employees and board members to seek jobs elsewhere, effectively collapsing the bank. It's a threat the hackers may never follow through on, yet it's damaging enough to just have that data. Releasing it to the public or to the highest bidder would cause severe-enough repercussions from all the local bank robbers everywhere to get the hackers the money they ask for, by an old-fashioned bank robbery, right? All without the hostage-taking. So why do they need a physical hostage?"

Jonas stepped in here to explain. "So far the hostages have all been released. Yet they are always hooded, if not drugged, so we get an anonymous tip, find them wandering an alleyway or a deserted street, with no knowledge of what happened to them, much less any idea of how the kidnapping happened or the vehicle involved or the men involved." Jonas shook his head. "It's pretty sophisticated for a kidnapping operation, especially where they have no need for the victim."

"But it's not a kidnapping operation in the end," Lachlan noted, frowning. "Surely hacking into all kinds of business ventures, banks and financial institutions, then just digitally locking everybody out of them for even a few minutes should be considered a serious crime. Regardless, the hackers are creating havoc and costing these companies serious money."

"And adding to those issues, in some cases, the ransom demand is almost nominal in some cases, especially compared to the damage that could result."

"It used to be nominal," Leah argued, "but it's not so nominal anymore."

"How much?" Lachlan asked.

"Unless you think twenty-five to fifty million dollars is *nominal* ..." She left it hanging in the air.

"No," Lachlan replied, cautiously feeling his way forward. "It's not, but neither is it enough to break even one medium-size bank."

"Exactly," Leah confirmed, "but it is an amount that

they could pay and keep everything still functioning."

"So, in that case, if the hackers needed to come back to the same bank at another time, they could," Lachlan theorized, with a sarcastic twist.

"And that is definitely one of the reasons why these boards of directors are so against paying out. They don't want to set a precedent that can then be repeated."

"How do they feel now, with the deaths of the CEOs?" Markus asked, a bit of an edge to his voice.

"The chairman who used his veto power to stop the payment on this last hacker demand is the one who was killed," she noted softly.

"And we're thinking that's deliberate?" Axel asked.

"It would appear so." Leah sighed. "I mean, … if you wanted to send a message, wouldn't you take out the biggest, baddest voice in the room?"

Lachlan nodded. "That would make sense, yes," he replied equally softly. "But the way they did it is also very interesting. Like a professional hit."

"Exactly," she agreed.

"So, what is it that you really want from us?" Markus asked, trying to get to her end game.

"I was hoping to quickly teach you some of the new programs that we're working with, then get your assistance on the current banking software systems," she explained. "We need to shore up any holes in their coding, maybe reinforce the back door with several layers of added protection. However, my team will deal with that, while I have you people out in the field, seeking anything suspicious. Who knows? You may find a drunk who saw something related to the local kidnapping or people physically scoping out the bank's comings and goings. Just keep your eyes and ears open. We need your people on the ground, and we need your people in the bank itself."

"*The* bank? Surely not the bank that's already been hit?" Lachlan asked, looking at her.

"No," she said, "but I have another one that I suspect will be hit next."

"Good," Lachlan noted. "I'd like to get ahead of these guys."

"The trouble is," she murmured, "I'm getting a little bit of static on my chosen bank."

"From the board? Is that it?" Markus asked.

"To a certain extent, yes ..." She hesitated, then continued. "It's also not one of the biggest banks around. It's more of a midsize bank. And, of course, I need access to bits and pieces of their banking system, and, given who I am, they don't want me anywhere near them."

Lachlan nodded ever-so-slightly at that. "So they're quite possibly scared that, if they give you access, you could potentially use it against them. For all they know, you could be somebody's way in."

"It's always great to know that I'm trusted *so very much*. Thanks for the reminder," she snapped testily.

"I think, in a situation such as this, nobody trusts anyone," Markus explained quietly.

Jonas, who had been silent so far, nodded. "I think that is quite a safe assumption," he agreed. "And, as much as I'm here to get information so we can solve this quickly, nothing about this case makes a whole lot of sense."

"Nothing about any of these related cases makes sense," she stated in exasperation.

Lachlan studied the area, as they walked out onto the main street. He understood he would be staying at the garrison overnight. He was tired, and they had been traveling all day. In a way, it seemed as if she had read his mind, as she looked over at him and shrugged.

"Sorry, things kind of blew up faster than expected," she stated. "No rest for the weary. We have to move quickly."

He nodded. "Something we're used to."

"I know," she murmured. "We did send an update back to your boss," she noted. "And, of course, I've updated Tesla."

"Is she on the hunt for whoever is doing the hacking?"

"She is," Leah confirmed, with a smile. "But she also wanted to get impressions from the field, as you guys moved on the ground."

"We can do that." Lachlan calmly assessed the group, getting nods from Jonas, Axel, and Markus, one by one. "Does Tesla have any theories to offer?" he asked Leah.

"Not that I've spoken about to her to date. She agrees with me on the next target though."

"That would be hugely helpful, if you're correct," Jonas added.

"The chances of it being correct are an issue for some." She nodded. "I get it, and believe me, I'm getting a lot of blowback from others because they don't agree. ... Yet I'm pretty sure I'm right, and, of course, there's no way to know until it actually happens."

With that, they had to be satisfied.

She pointed out a vehicle ahead of them—a large SUV, with smoky windows.

Lachlan smiled. "Government-issue vehicles all look the same, no matter where we are."

She chuckled. "Yeah, they sure do. They're probably even built by the same companies."

And, with that, they climbed into the twin back seats.

She sat in the middle of Lachlan and Jonas. "Jonas, I am surprised that you're here right now."

"Hey, I need to know what you guys know," he stated bluntly. "We've got people dying on English soil, and that's never something that will go down well in my world. The fact that it's being done across Europe just means that we need to all be on the same page. Interpol is in the loop at every step as well."

"Oh, I agree completely," she murmured. "Though it isn't necessarily *all* across Europe," she noted cautiously. "However, there is a chance that's where the hackers are going, and we do want to stop it before it gets any worse."

"Agreed," Jonas replied, a tinge of anger to his tone.

"You're just pissed because they headed into England first, aren't you?" Markus teased, with a smile.

"Not so much that they went there first," Jonas argued, "but that they went there at all."

Lachlan looked over at him. "You did come pretty quickly though, didn't you?"

"I wouldn't miss it," Jonas teased. "I knew you were coming."

"You wouldn't miss the chance to show off," Lachlan suggested, with a big fat grin.

"What better way to keep track of what goes on?" Jonas admitted. "We all know that the person here at the information spot gets the best details."

"But these aren't the good details to be had," Leah noted, her voice hard. "We have real families being affected by this."

Jonas had the grace to look ashamed. "And I'm not trying to minimize that," he responded quietly. "We're all more than fed up with this whole thing too."

"Of course you are." She turned her gaze to stare through the tinted glass. "And what you all should probably know—right now, instead of down the road—is that the last person who was killed … was someone I knew."

LEAH STOPPED, CLEARED her throat. "And a good friend, which just made this all the more personal." Before any of them had a chance to react, the vehicle took several sharp turns, sending her careening off to the side. She immediately turned to look at the two men in the front seat. "Is there a problem?" she asked, leaning forward and directing her inquiry to the guy in the passenger seat.

The driver had no name to go with the face in her mind. Neither did his passenger, who shook his head. "I don't think so," he replied calmly, but he was studying the rearview mirror and his side mirror.

"We *are* being followed," Lachlan declared, as the SUV made more drastic changes, and he shifted on his seat.

She looked at him, still unsure what to think of this trio from Mason's team, even though she'd already been well prepped by Tesla. Leah had been given a concise description of exactly who these men were, but, at the same time, she preferred to make her own assessments. She asked Lachlan, "How can you tell for sure?"

"Because the driver is maneuvering to get rid of them." Lachlan flashed a smile, pointing to the guy in the front seat. "The same black SUV has been behind us for quite a while."

At that, the driver looked back at him. "Did you get a decent glimpse at it?"

"No, not yet," he replied. "I presume you don't know

who they are."

"No, I sure don't," he stated. "But this is one of their latest tactics. Taking down people before they get a chance to know they are a target."

"Interesting, but that also means they are far-reaching, as in we just flew in to Germany."

"Very much so. Must be an international group or one with great online resources."

With that, Lachlan went quiet again, but his gaze never left the trailing vehicle. Their ride suddenly took a hard left, careening around the corner again. Leah swayed badly, and other men reacted more assuredly around her. She didn't have much chance other than to hold on to both Jonas and Lachlan.

She spent her life on computers and delving into software systems and online research, so this was a little out of her usual realm. And she couldn't ignore the fact that Lachlan had immediately placed his arm in front of her to stop her from falling to the floor.

Even though she was buckled in, his move obviously was an instinctive reaction on his part. She shook her head at that and held on to him for a moment longer.

"Are you okay?" he whispered.

She took a deep breath. "This is a little out of my comfort zone," she murmured.

He nodded. "It's out of almost everyone's comfort zones," he noted, with an engaging grin.

And that damn grin definitely hit the right chord.

The fact that Tesla had warned Leah about that grin was something else, but she thought that maybe she was immune to his charms. She had more confidence in herself, especially when she'd been warned about it. But apparently not. She found herself instinctively responding in the same way. "This seems to be pretty normal for you."

"I don't know about normal, but it's definitely something I have experience with," he murmured.

"Good for you," she admitted. "I'm okay if I don't ever have an experience like this."

At that, he burst out laughing. The vehicle then took another sharp turn, and, once again, she was up against his strong arm, as he held her in place. "I do have on a seat belt, you know?" she mentioned mildly.

"Yep, and you can get a hell of a nasty bruise from the belt if you hit up against it hard as we take these corners. Something about force and inertia," he noted, without even turning to look at her.

She pondered that for a moment, and then realized he was probably correct. And it was not worthwhile to argue. Besides, to know that somebody cared enough about her to ignore getting hurt to keep her in place was unsettling and yet comforting. Now whether that was because he was also somebody Tesla liked or just part of his protective personality, Leah didn't know, but she wasn't used to having someone look after her. Yet it really wasn't the time to sit here and argue about it either.

Suddenly the vehicle took another series of sharp turns. She held her breath, noting that this got more serious. She sat up a bit and looked out the back window, when Lachlan immediately grabbed her head and told her to stay down. She looked at him for a moment, not comprehending, as he kept her head down and urged her to stay there.

As soon as she was about to ask him to let her go, she heard gunfire. She stared at him, wordless, but he was down with her. Almost immediately he popped up and said, "Nice.

Bulletproof glass."

"I didn't even know we had that feature," she whispered.

"Doesn't matter," he noted quietly. "It's all good."

She wasn't so sure about that, but this was definitely more than she had bargained for today. She closed her eyes and whispered a silent prayer to get them out of this. When the vehicle slowed down and came to another sharp corner and then hit the brakes hard, she looked over at Lachlan.

"I'd say we're here," he noted, with a grin.

She stared at that grin suspiciously. "Did you enjoy that?"

"Hey, nothing like a welcome like that to make you feel at home."

She snorted. "Since when is that a great welcome?" Lachlan quickly unbuckled her seat belt and ushered her out the door of the SUV. She asked, "Are we even supposed to be leaving the vehicle?" But then she noted the other men were outside already, handguns at the ready, even though they were surrounded by three closed-in walls to a carport-type area, with a town house above. "Where are we?" she asked.

"A safe house," one of guys replied evenly. "Let's get you inside."

"Why are we parked outside?" she asked.

Lachlan chuckled. "The drivers will immediately get us new wheels."

She was led into the garage and to an elevator at the far back wall and then upstairs. As she stepped into the building, she looked around at the empty anteroom and frowned. "I don't even know where we are."

"It's better this way," noted the driver and his partner, as they came up behind her. "Someone is a little too interested in us."

Everybody gathered together, and nobody moved farther inside.

"On whose orders are we here?" she asked calmly, but calmness had nothing to do with what was going through her mind. She was beyond freaked out.

"This is where we were ordered to bring you if we were followed, and then, with the gunfire, it became imperative," the driver explained. "It is plain and simple that somebody may be trying to ensure you don't live long enough to untangle this mess. Meanwhile, the rest of us will keep you alive. So you're welcome."

"I appreciate the effort," she replied, reaching up a shaky hand. "I can't say that was a trip I'm ever likely to forget."

Lachlan grinned at her. "You're safe here, but we'll do a full reconnaissance."

At that, Markus stepped up. "I'll go."

Lachlan gave him a nod. "We can use the extra hands." He looked over at Axel and asked, "You coming or staying?"

"I'm staying behind with Leah and you guys," he replied. "We've got three to hunt already."

Jonas nodded. "That's fair."

"Don't worry, Jonas," Lachlan added. "We'll find them. They won't get her."

"Good," Jonas stated. "She's the only one who has figured out this much about what the hell's going on."

"By the way, who else would know that?" Lachlan asked suddenly, staring at all gathered here.

The driver looked at him, confused, then realized what he meant and nodded. "I don't know, but that's a good question, and we need to find the answer to it." And, with that, he and his partner and Markus were gone.

She looked at the three men still here. "I don't understand what's going on."

"That was either an attempt to kidnap you or an attempt to see just how serious we were about this op," Lachlan noted.

"Why would anybody try to kidnap me?" she asked, astounded.

"Because you are the analyst helping the banks sort this out," Axel explained quietly.

She shook her head. "But that's just crazy. I don't know anything about this case yet. There is absolutely nothing concrete that I could find to date."

"Maybe you did find something," Lachlan suggested, "but aren't giving it enough importance. You said yourself you have a plausible location for the next attack. You sounded pretty certain about it."

"I may be certain and yet proven wrong very shortly." She stared at Lachlan slowly and then nodded her head. "But you do realize what that means."

"Insiders, I know." Lachlan's tone was equally grim. "Do you realize what that means?"

"Sure," she acknowledged. "It means that somebody has figured out I am on the right track and that person is passing along information."

"I'll go with passing information," Lachlan agreed immediately. "Guys like this, they'll pay very well."

She shook her head. "That's not nice," she muttered. "I work as part of a team."

"And has that team been vetted?"

"I'm sure it was, as far as I knew."

"Does Tesla know this team?"

"Not personally, no," Leah admitted. "They were given to me."

"Maybe it's a good time to take a serious look at who you've been working with."

"I did back then, when I first got on board," she stated, then she frowned. "However, we have had a couple changes in staff."

"Anyway you look at it, we need to be objective here. Everyone in your inner circle gets a second look."

She nodded carefully. "Except for the fact that I'm no longer at my office. Therefore, I can't get into our computer systems."

"Can a laptop give you the access you need?"

She stared at him for a long moment, then nodded. "I guess I just don't want to be stuck here for very long."

"None of us do," Axel stated, as they walked through an inner door and entered a small apartment.

She looked around. "I don't even understand what this is."

Axel laughed to help dispel her uneasiness. "It's a safe house, and we have lots of them all around Europe, but this one? … This one isn't ours."

Lachlan wandered through it, nodded, and added, "Doesn't really matter though. They're all the same, aren't they?" He looked over at Axel, who nodded.

"Seems like it," he agreed. "Once you've been in one, it appears as though you've been in them all."

"I didn't really need this experience to begin with," she groaned.

"But now that you're here," Lachlan stated, with a smile, "it's all good."

"Says you," she muttered, "but I don't like anything about it." She slumped into a chair in the living room and asked, "Now what?"

CHAPTER 2

A S LEAH LOOKED at the facial expressions of the men, she realized that not one of them had a ready response. When she considered her question, it was absurd to even ask. At least so soon after an attempt on them—or her. First, they had been following orders. Second, they had just arrived.

She shook her head. "I shouldn't even be asking you that. I should be finding out myself."

"Then you better find something quick," Lachlan noted agreeably, "and let us know."

She glared at him, not wanting to be reasonable at all. "I just want to go back to my place."

"Is that where you were planning on going before?"

"No. I was taking you to headquarters."

"Who would know that?"

"Anybody who knew you guys were coming," she snapped, "and that would be a lot of people."

"When you say *a lot*, how many is that?" he asked immediately.

"Better yet, how long would it take to get a closer look at that lot?" Jonas asked behind her.

She reached up a hand. "Not that long," she admitted. "I mean, a lot would be at least a dozen. And maybe not even that." She was sure it was close to that.

"Who else would know?" Jonas asked.

"The drivers' bosses maybe," she suggested, looking around. Then she frowned. "I didn't know either man, did you?"

"No," Jonas replied.

The other men responded with headshakes of their own, then Lachlan looked at her and smiled. "How about some coffee?" Then he motioned around her. "This place should be fully equipped."

"If you know how to make some, that would be great," she muttered.

He burst out laughing. "I think I can manage it, if anything's here to work with. While we do that, why don't you see if you can get word of what's expected of us from here on out."

"Right." She pulled out her phone. Several attempts to get through were unsuccessful. Then she looked around. "Do you think we're in a special shielded area because I can't get reception here."

He nodded. "That would be quite likely."

"Great," she muttered. Just then, her phone rang. "Well, somebody can get through," she muttered in surprise.

"That's not all that unusual," Jonas noted simply.

She stared at him, shook her head, and answered her phone. "Hey, boss." She paused as he spoke to her. "Yes, we're all safe. Three guys have gone out, looking for more bad guys. The rest of us are trying to figure out if there's coffee to be had." She smiled at hearing her boss's loud noisy exhale of relief.

"Not to mention food," Lachlan chipped in, while sorting through the kitchen cupboards.

"Yes, I know. I've been up all night and feel the same way." She listened to her boss for a moment, adding, "No,

I'll tell him." She hung up. "We're here temporarily, until they can figure out whether it's safe to bring us into our scheduled accommodations."

"Our scheduled accommodations?" Lachlan asked, looking over at her, his eyebrows raised.

She nodded. "Yes, I had made arrangements to stay with your team during this whole scenario," she shared, lost in thought for a moment, "at least until we get to the bottom of it."

"Interesting," Lachlan noted. "I'm sure that didn't go down too well with your family. No pets?"

"Not here. And not until I'm more settled. I love cats and will get one or two down the road. I was raised with several. However as much as I loved them, I'm under no misunderstanding about their rulership over us all."

At that, Lachlan burst out laughing. "Oh my, I love cats too, but there is something about that very independent personality."

"Regardless I do love them. It's not the easiest to live without furry friends especially after a lifetime of having them close."

"I can imagine," Lachlan agreed. "They do give back a lot of that love."

"All the time." She looked around. "Did you give up on the coffee?"

Lachlan grinned at her. "No. I've got a pot dripping."

"I figured they would have one of those machines with the pods," she noted.

"That would be simpler in a way, but this regular coffee machine makes twelve cups at a time, which we'll go through quickly enough," he replied. "Plus I figured that we would all need some as we make plans." He turned toward Axel. "Your thoughts?"

"Yeah." Axel's voice was hard and unyielding. "I want a full investigation into everybody who knew that we were coming in today. I want to know everything and everybody involved in any way, no exceptions."

"Ditto," Leah agreed calmly. "I'm racking my brain right now, trying to figure out who could have been behind this."

"I think," Axel stated, "we're pretty sure it'll be related to the banking scenario, but, most important, we need to figure this the crap out and soon. ... We need to know who's got a line into your own team."

"We can't just blame my team," she protested immediately.

"No, we can't, but it's a really good place to start." Axel kept his stare firmly on her.

She glared back at Axel. "It might be a place to start, but it won't be the place we end."

"Maybe not," he agreed, "but let's at least rule them out in an objective manner. This isn't the time to be emotionally vested," he told her calmly, "and we do have secure internet here."

"I saw that." She waved her phone. "I still don't have my laptop."

"No, but we have laptops and a computer system here," he noted, "if you want to come see."

She stared at him, hopped up quickly, then followed Axel. "Is this place equipped?"

"They often are," he stated, "and there should be a full gamut of weapons here as well." He looked over at Jonas. "Thoughts?"

"Hey, I'm just waiting for you guys to do your thing," he replied. "Every time you come to my country, you just pull this shit out of the air and make my life hell. I figured you'd do the same in this case. So I figured I'd get a jump on the shit show if I came early to watch and to learn."

At that, Axel grinned. "Hey, I don't think it's quite so simple as that."

"It always has been before," Jonas muttered. He walked over, pulled off a dust cover to a desktop computer, and nodded. "Wow, that's way too similar to ours at MI6. I wonder if the same guy designs these?" he asked in a hard voice.

"Something like that wouldn't be at all surprising," Lachlan noted, as he stepped up. He pulled a small desk away from the wall and it opened up into an alcove. In it was a state-of-the-art computer system with several modules.

What she saw left her absolutely stunned. She looked at him and smiled. "Now this is more like it. At least maybe I can get some information from here."

"If nothing else," Lachlan added, "maybe let Tesla know what's going on."

"I already sent her a text," Leah replied. "As soon as I had service, I updated her on the situation."

"Interesting how the internet works here," Jonas muttered. "But at least it does work—somewhat."

"Yeah, and only because I changed one of the ports on the router," Axel noted. "I've been in a couple safe houses myself. If you don't know how they function, it's easy to waste time, and we don't have any time to lose."

"You think?" she quipped, as she walked over to the computers, took a closer look, and immediately snagged a gaming setup that appealed to her and started pounding on the keyboard.

First, she had to see what the log-ins looked like to determine whether they had security here or not. Satisfied that she could get in and out of where she needed to go without leaving a trace, she immediately set up a blind, so nobody could follow her tracks, then sent off emails.

"You'll wipe that when you're done, right?" Lachlan asked, from beside her.

"It'll do it automatically," she replied, barely taking any interest in what he was saying.

He stared at her. "Another little Tesla trick?"

"It's one that a lot of us use," she said, with a laugh, dragging her gaze to him and smiling at the look on his face. "It's not necessarily something that we share with other people."

"Of course not," he noted. "All you cyberpeople are so security conscious."

"Now you know why," she stated, raising an eyebrow. "You all want me to find answers, yet I'll need a minute."

"You got a minute," he agreed patiently.

When she turned around again, he held out a cup of coffee for her. She laughed as she took it, yet sent a head nod in his direction. "That's not helpful."

"What?"

"Hovering much?"

"Not much. Have you found anything helpful?" Lachlan asked, ignoring the jab.

"Nope, not yet," she replied. "I'm getting there though. Tesla's up to speed, Rob has agreed that we should stay here. Even though I'm not sure that it's necessarily what I want to do."

"Oh, I get it," he noted. "Back to that whole independence thing again."

"No," she groaned. "It's just back to having my life, but

I already agreed that I would stay until this mess was sorted," she confirmed. "So it won't make a whole lot of difference whether it's here or in a hotel."

"Probably safer here," he noted.

"I think that's what they're all leading to. It's just not my idea of great accommodations."

"I think it's meant to sleep six," Jonas stated, as he joined them. "Which is plenty for us."

"So you're staying here too?" she asked, staring at him with a narrow gaze.

He gave her a fat smile. "I'm part of this, whether you like it or not."

She thought about that for a moment. "Fine, but somebody needs to cook because I'm hungry, and there's no food. I swear to God I haven't eaten a thing since this morning, as I was expecting to get food as soon as we got settled."

"As a matter of fact," Lachlan added, "that was on our mind too. We thought we would figure it out at the regularly scheduled accommodations."

"That's out the window," she stated.

"We noticed," Jonas quipped.

Jonas was not letting her have the final word on anything. He was assertive, cocky, and far too arrogant for his own damn good.

"That's much appreciated," Lachlan said, interrupting whatever was starting between Jonas and Leah. "At least this way, Jonas, you're on the spot and will be getting as much information on this as you can."

"Of course," she agreed, "but *I* don't have to be here for that. With my laptop, I can theoretically work anywhere."

"And we have laptops here that you can work on wherever as well. However, I think somebody probably wants you more than they want any of us," Lachlan reminded her, as he sat down beside her.

"You're just guessing at that," she argued. "There's no reason for anybody to be after me more than any one of you guys. I'm certain you each have made plenty of enemies."

"Again we're back to you deliberately not seeing the value that you are as a target," Lachlan repeated. "And, even if the gathered data is only to be destroyed, you have information that other people will want."

At that, Jonas nodded. "I agree with Lachlan actually, and the fact that it happened while you were with us means they are after you, not the rest of us. No one will care that we just arrived, and frankly we probably just look like henchmen, if nothing else."

"How can you say that?"

"No matter what you think, there is a possibility that you are in danger."

"Maybe, but …" She shook her head. "Tons of people know who you are. I'm sure your face raised all kinds of flags."

"Yeah, and probably made a lot of people laugh to think the gunmen sent MI6 scurrying to Germany," he stated in disgust.

"That could have just been a power play," Leah noted.

"The other thing to consider is," Lachlan added, as he looked at them, "that their little ploy to come after us didn't succeed. What it did do was send us running to a safe house, and they likely have a good idea of approximately where we are, within a certain radius. So the question really is, was that the end result they wanted, or did they want to take us down?"

"Another question to ask is, did they really want to capture us or did they just want to send us running? And, if so, have we just played into their hands?" Jonas chipped in cheerfully.

She stared at him, frowning. "Which means that they're out there, waiting for us."

"Yes, that would be my guess," Jonas replied.

"What about the men?" she asked in shock. "What about Markus and the others, the two drivers?"

"I don't know." Jonas looked at her. "Have you got any way to communicate with the drivers?"

"Don't you?" she challenged.

"I tried to contact Markus a couple times," Lachlan interjected, "but got no answer."

She stared at him, a sick feeling in her stomach. "That's not cool."

"I trust Markus completely," he murmured, "and, if he has any idea that he's being followed or suspects he's compromised in any way, he will not come back here. No way he would take a chance on leading danger back to us."

"Yet that won't be helpful," she noted, "because we'll need his help."

"Not necessarily," Lachlan pointed out. "Maybe he's better off at headquarters, ... doing what he came to do, which is working on some of the computers."

She glared at him. "Yeah, but he was supposed to be working with me."

"He still can, but he just might have to do it remotely, from where he is."

"Shit," she muttered. "I need my team."

"And you may not be getting that team," Jonas stated. "I'm guessing that the minute anybody realizes someone has been compromised, that entire team will be cut out of the loop, while we figure out what's going on."

She winced. "Damn. That's exactly what I would suggest, ... if somebody had asked me," she muttered. "I just don't want to think about it happening to me right now."

LACHLAN NOTED THAT Leah was in a state of crisis, where outrage, confusion, and a little bit of fear had her ready to jump at the smallest *click*. At the same time, her anger flared that somebody could have done this ... on purpose. But she was also working her way through it, and Lachlan had to appreciate that. Not everybody was exposed to danger—and certainly not all the time—but, even when they were, it always came down to how they handled it.

So far she was doing just fine, at least in his opinion. When his phone buzzed, he looked down to see a message from Tesla sitting on his screen.

Status.

She was quick and asking for an update, when he had nothing to report. He quickly responded. **Everyone is fine that we know of. Markus is out hunting. Haven't had any contact.** Then he sent a follow-up. **Could be on purpose.**

Immediately Tesla's reply came. **It is. I've had contact. As of ten minutes ago, he was fine.**

He smiled at that.

"What?" Leah asked.

"Tesla heard from Markus."

"That's good," Leah noted. "What's going on?"

Another text from Tesla came in, giving him a bit more information. "So far they're doing a full search outside. Nobody's seen anything, and the following vehicle is gone, but it looks like they're not coming back here. And Markus doesn't want to take a chance on leading them here at this point. He's heading back to the original destination," Lachlan shared, "which looks like a name I can't even pronounce."

"Yes. Heard that one before." She waved her hand at him. "He'll go back to the hotel, get a nice shower, and have a hot dinner."

He looked up, his lips quirking. "Hey, it's a nice gig, if you can get it."

She stared at him. "You're not at all bothered about staying here?" she asked. "Then again I said here or there didn't matter either, didn't I?"

"Nope, I'm okay regardless. Like you said, here is as good as anywhere," he agreed. "And, if we don't have food, we'll find a way to get some." He looked over at Axel. "Suggestions?"

"We're not going anywhere," Axel replied, "but a delivery will be coming soon enough. When we're in a safe house, the point is to stay inside. Our guys out there are trying to make sure this location is secure, and we will do our part and stay put."

"So, maybe for tonight," Lachlan offered, "we'll see what there might be to cook." With that discussion concluded, Axel disappeared into the other room.

She watched Axel leave. "Everybody appears to be so calm," she marveled, "as if this were so commonplace."

"Most of us, even Jonas, have been in many scenarios far worse than this," Lachlan stated simply. "We're not being hunted out on the streets, so that counts for something. We're in a place where we are safe and where we can keep track of what's going on. We also have communications," he noted, "which is huge. So the fact that we might be a little short on food is really not a big deal." At that, her stomach growled so loud that he burst out laughing. "Okay, ... so, for you, maybe food is a big deal."

"It's not even that it's a big deal," she replied sadly. "It's just a scenario that I'm not necessarily used to."

"Got it." Lachlan nodded. "And this kind of thing is something you don't want to get used to anyway. So let's dig down, dig deep, and see what the hell is going on. Then we can get out of here all that much sooner."

She sighed. "Sounds good to me. Unfortunately I'm not sure it will be all that easy."

"Why is that?"

"Because they'll keep us pinned down here, and we're the ones who are now in trouble. So let me ask, what are the chances of anybody even listening to me about where I think the next attack will be?" she asked quietly.

"Do you really think the fact that you were targeted will cause anybody to *not* believe the information you've got?" he asked curiously. "Wouldn't it *make* them believe it that much more?"

"I don't know," she replied, with a frown. "It doesn't feel like it though."

Lachlan shared a look with Jonas, who had rejoined them. She was making assumptions, and that would not sit well with any of them. Rationality was their only true friend, and they had all been around the block enough to make their own judgments.

Jonas nodded. "It should make them believe it all the more," he confirmed. "And, even if your team doesn't want the information, I do. We'll try to get a scenario sorted and set up a sting very quickly."

"Maybe," she reluctantly acknowledged. "I know they had plans to set up a defensive system, but we don't have time now."

"What makes you think timing is an issue?"

Just then Lachlan heard Axel calling for him from the kitchen. Lachlan turned and left quickly, and, as soon as he walked in and saw Axel standing in front of the fridge, Lachlan knew the reason for the emergency help. "Yes, I can cook," Lachlan stated immediately.

Axel nodded. "Good, but I wanted to tell you that I just heard from Markus."

With his voice lowered, though Lachlan wasn't exactly sure why, he leaned forward. "Okay. Any problems?"

"He'll tell everybody he's heading back to the hotel, but he'll keep watch outside instead. He figures that we're under surveillance, and he wants to figure out who it is and why."

"Good enough," Lachlan replied. "We can relieve him in a few hours and set it up on a regular schedule."

"I suggested that to him, but he was fairly noncommittal. He actually said, 'We'll see.'"

Lachlan laughed at that. "Is there anything he likes better than being outside in the action?"

"Being home with his wife," Axel replied, with a grin.

"Is that him or you? But, hey, you guys all have partners. I don't, but I do understand the draw, after watching everybody pairing up," he admitted.

"Don't worry," Axel murmured. "It'll happen for you in good time."

"Maybe, maybe not," he replied, clearly changing the conversation. "Anyway I won't worry about it. Food first."

At that, Axel pulled some hamburger from the freezer. "Everything is frozen, but we should do some pasta or something with this."

"Good enough," Lachlan agreed. "We can do spaghetti." As he walked over to the pantry and pulled out some pasta and canned pasta sauce, he asked, "Is anything fresh in there?"

"Not a whole lot. I don't think they were expecting us."

Lachlan poked his head into the fridge, found bottled water and a few soft drinks. That was it. "We should have a delivery coming too," Lachlan added, "but not in time for tonight's dinner. Let's just make some food, have some coffee, and see what kind of information we can roust up."

"And, if Markus finds something, that would be interesting."

"Trust Markus to be where the action is."

CHAPTER 3

B Y THE TIME Leah lifted her head from the computer, her eyes burned, and she had a headache. Her first thought that came to mind was food, but she didn't want to hassle anybody about it. It seemed like they were all pretty calm and contained about the whole scenario, making her feel like she was the only one struggling.

But then, she was. And it was hard to not make some comment about it too. However, she was alone in the computer room at the moment. Getting up, she stretched, then wandered toward the kitchen, where she found Axel and Lachlan working away. She stopped in the middle of the room and asked, "Is there anything I can do to help?"

Lachlan looked up at her and smiled. "Hey, you look like you're about ready to crash."

"Yep," Axel agreed, looking at her with a grin.

"I have to admit that I'm pretty well frazzled," she stated. "I've been working steadily for the last couple days."

"The food will be ready in a few minutes," Lachlan shared. "So, if you want to help, how about you set the table?"

Not sure what they were having to eat, she was willing to give it a shot. She immediately pulled out dishes and brought over plates and cutlery, then located the salt and pepper after that. She quickly had it all set up, before crashing onto a chair in front of them. "What's for dinner?" she asked, curiously sniffing the air.

"Pasta." Lachlan turned toward her, smiled, and asked, "You don't have any food issues, do you?"

"Should have thought of that before," Axel chipped in.

"Only that I'm always hungry," she replied. "But no allergies, sensitivities, or particular aversions, if that's what you meant."

"Good thing," Lachlan stated cheerfully, as he set a platter in front of her on the table, and very quickly she had her plate full of spaghetti.

"Considering no fresh food was to be had here, you've done a pretty good job."

"There'll be fresh food tomorrow," Lachlan noted.

"Do you think they'll take the chance of bringing us something?" she asked. "I don't know how the whole safe house thing works."

"They will," Jonas agreed, as he sat down beside her.

She looked over at him in surprise. "Oh, hello, Jonas. I'd forgotten you were here."

He chuckled. "I had a bit of a nap. I was at the crime scene most of the night." He sniffed the air appreciatively. "Hey, and I really do like the fact that you guys can cook. That'll make this a whole lot easier."

Jonas could be quite charming when he needed to be. "Of course, and a food delivery is coming," Lachlan shared, with a look at her.

"We'll get a delivery," Axel stated, with a shrug. "Otherwise I can certainly do a grocery run."

"And how do you keep our location a secret if that's the case?" she asked.

He chuckled. "It's not a problem," he murmured. "And

let's not forget Markus is out there too."

Leah turned to Lachlan, a confused expression on her face. "He is? I thought he'd gone to the hotel." He quickly updated her. "Okay, so that is something we have to change. No holding back information. I thought he was at the hotel, enjoying luxurious accommodations."

"Nope, he changed his mind," Lachlan added. "He was hoping to see if he could spot somebody watching us."

"Well, fine," she muttered, "but who'll relieve him?"

"Maybe nobody," Axel replied. "He's pretty stubborn."

"He also shouldn't be out there all on his own for the whole time." Leah stared at Axel, then Lachlan and Jonas. They just silently looked at her, until finally she raised both hands in surrender. "Fine. I'm just the analyst. What do I know?" After a big yawn, her attention returned to her plate. She wasn't even a few bites in, when she had to stop. "I must say, this is quite good. My compliments to the chef."

Axel and Lachlan looked at each other, then shrugged. "We'll take it," Lachlan said, with a grin.

"You're welcome," Axel added.

She smiled at them. "You guys are so much like the rest of Mason's team."

"Do you know them?" Lachlan asked her.

"A lot of them," she confirmed. "Whenever I'm in the US, I tend to spend a fair bit of time over at Tesla's place. At least until I feel like I'm in the way, and then I kick myself out."

"I highly doubt that happens very often."

"The problem is, Tesla and I can get very involved in our work, on some of our side projects," she explained. "So it's pretty common for Mason to call it quits and to tell us to stop talking shop." At that, they just stared at her. She shrugged. "I mean, I can't really blame him."

"Maybe not," Axel replied, staring at her. "Yet he's pretty bad for talking shop himself."

"Of course," she admitted. "But all this cyberstuff isn't necessarily his cup of tea."

At that, they laughed. "Nope. He likes his computers just fine, but I suspect you two geeks probably take it to a whole new level."

"Yep, we sure do, but that's also where we're most comfortable." At that, she looked over at Jonas, who was eating steadily. "Are you even breathing between bites?" she asked, with a teasing note.

He looked up and smiled. "I'm not particularly bothered about breathing. It's good food, and I don't know when I'll get my next meal."

She stared at him in shock. "Really?"

He shrugged. "I've been in this job way too long, and there's absolutely no way to know when we'll be discovered. So I plan on being prepared and ready to go all the damn time."

"So that's why you've had your beauty sleep already then."

"Yep," he agreed, "and I've already contacted MI6 headquarters and let them know what's happened. They're not impressed, and, as a matter of fact, I think they would like me to come home. Except they know that I'm better off right here now, while this chaos is going on. We were targeted. Or rather somebody in that vehicle was targeted. My guess is it was you, but they don't want to take any chances. So it looks like I'm here for the duration."

"Good," she noted. "I realize that not everybody likes you all that much"—then she frowned—"or at least I think a lot of people don't like you."

At that, Jonas gave her a big fat grin. "Believe me. You're not the first person to tell me that, mostly because they stomp around in my backyard, without so much as a care for all the trouble they cause me."

"That's not very nice of them, is it?" she asked, speaking extra sweetly and completely ignoring Axel and Lachlan.

"Nope, not at all." Jonas chuckled. "And, to make matters worse, I don't think they care."

"Come on, Jonas. You know what it's like when you're on a mission," Axel argued. "You got to do what you got to do."

"But you people seem to always do it in a way that leaves the rest of us cleaning up your messes," Jonas complained, with an eye roll.

"It's not that bad," Axel argued, with a smirk.

"Besides, it's not just us who you have a problem with," Lachlan added. "It's Levi, Ice, and their team too, right?"

"Sometimes," he admitted. "And honestly it's not even just them personally. It's the shit you all pull. I mean, I've got Terk sometimes leading me on a merry chase. Before I even have a chance to find out it's him or to confirm anything is going on, some bizarre problem is dropped in my lap. It seems the whole bunch of them knows things I've never even heard about." Jonas raised both hands in frustration.

"Oh, man, I've heard rumors about Terk," Leah shared immediately, "but I've never met him."

"And you might not ever see him," Jonas noted. "If there was ever a ghost, it's that one."

"So I've heard." Leah seemed more excited about the whole concept than anything.

Jonas had to laugh at her. "Terk is a character and a half. But, if you think you know anything about him, you'd be wrong," he murmured. "He's fast, and he's knowledgeable, but he's also scary as hell."

"I have heard that too." Leah smiled. "But, hey, at least he's on our side."

"There is that," Jonas agreed, with a nod.

Smiling, she looked back at Lachlan and Axel. "Thank you for making dinner. It was delicious."

"You're welcome. Is everybody finished?" Lachlan asked, looking at the others.

"I am, and now I think I'll go crash for a little bit," Leah noted. "I'll get up and get back to work as soon as I've had a chance to close my eyes." With that, she rose, carried her dishes to the sink, and washed her plate in the hot soapy water already waiting for her, wondering at these men who could cook and clean and keep a safe house completely calm, without any evidence of stress. Then she turned to look around. "Jonas, which bedroom did you take?"

"Top left," he replied. "Pick another and you're good to go."

With that, she nodded and headed upstairs. At least the guys had luggage because they had just been picked up from their travels. She had nothing, not even a toothbrush. What she'd really like was a shower and a change of clothes, but that wasn't likely to happen either.

She chose a bedroom at random, figuring as long as it appeared to be empty that she was probably okay to claim it as her own. She walked into the bathroom, used the facilities, and then walked over to the bed, pulling the blanket back off the top sheet and just crashed underneath, the blanket over her shoulders.

What a strange day and a strange scenario she had been caught up in. She knew the only way to get her life back was to get some rest and to hit it again later on.

LACHLAN STOOD IN the hallway, watching which bedroom she chose, checking out her demeanor as she closed the door behind her. She hadn't even looked around, so it was good. She felt safe, but, at the same time, she was probably too exhausted to do much anyway. He returned to the kitchen to finish cleaning up, even as he found Jonas washing up his dishes.

"Is she okay?" Jonas asked.

"Exhausted and stressed mostly. She didn't collapse during the gunfire, and she appears to have held her own in terms of shock and adrenaline," Lachlan pointed out.

"I wasn't sure how all that would go down."

"We never are, it seems."

"But she's a civilian, somebody with tremendous computer skills," Jonas noted.

"Strange that she doesn't seem to think she has any value as a hostage though," Lachlan mentioned.

"Honestly she would be a huge asset if they kidnapped her, if for no other reason than the ransom she could bring to try to keep her safe," Jonas added, looking pensive.

"Much more likely that they would have just killed her," Axel argued. "And yet you notice that none of the attacks on us were anything to that level."

"I wondered about that," Jonas admitted. "They could have completely annihilated us out there on the road with enough overwhelming firepower or with just one massive warhead on a rocket. And I suspect this group would have had the money and the means to do so."

"So, why didn't they?" Axel asked him.

"I don't know."

"That's something we have to get to the bottom of," Axel stated, "and she's not at all happy about us investigating her team."

"I don't think that she has a choice in the matter," Lachlan noted.

"Not only is there no choice," Jonas added, "but we need to finish whatever you started."

"I'm good with that."

"Yeah?"

"We are," Lachlan repeated, with a smile. "So is Tesla. Somebody knew we were coming."

"You guys traveled by military aircraft, so there would be military records."

"Sure," Lachlan agreed. "All kinds of records would reveal that we were all coming this way."

"I came over on a commercial flight," Jonas noted, with a shrug, "and wasn't trying to hide my identity."

"Another valid point," Lachlan stated, "and I really don't think any of us were the intended target, so it all goes back to Leah. We've got to find out who knew she was coming to pick us up and if somebody knew beforehand that the hackers were trying to stop her."

"Did they just ask about her itinerary? Maybe what she was doing today, as far as work went? Like was it not even an issue? Because, if you think about it, she seems pretty casual about the whole thing."

"That's because she doesn't deal with this cloak-and-dagger stuff like we do," Axel murmured. "I think she's just clueless about the fact that she's been targeted."

"Having those blinders on won't work very long for me," Jonas declared. "We need to get to the bottom of this and fast."

"Which is also why Tesla's on it too," Lachlan shared.

At that, Jonas frowned. "I've heard a lot about this Tesla person."

"Yeah, and your chances to get to know her better are not very good. Nonexistent, I would say."

"I know," Jonas agreed. "Mason's not very fond of traveling for pleasure, just because he knows what goes on and how many adversaries they have made worldwide."

"So, you think they'll avoid England because of that?" Lachlan asked, with an eye roll.

"I just think, at the moment, they're not traveling very far at all. Maybe that makes more sense than anything," Jonas suggested. "Besides, if she's the kind of person who's always involved in her work, then she probably doesn't want to leave the office very much either."

"No, she really doesn't travel much," Lachlan noted. "But times change, so who knows."

But then the conversation moved to Markus. "I'll go out and relieve him," Axel stated, as he tossed a tea towel onto the counter. "He can at least come in and get some food, and, if he's insistent on going back out afterward, he can."

"Good enough." Lachlan sat again and waited. It wasn't long before a knock came that he recognized. He got up and let Markus in. "Hey, anything going on?"

"No," he replied. "Really quiet out there."

Markus looked over at Jonas and frowned, and Jonas immediately frowned back. "Yeah, I know," Jonas replied. "I'm not your favorite person."

Markus just smiled, his face split with the biggest grin.

"Hey, I'm not in England, so I don't have to hide my presence or even let you know where I'm at. So it's all good," Jonas rolled his eyes at that. "Like you would anyway."

"I would try," Markus quipped. "We don't go into your country deliberately trying to pull shit on you. ... You know that, right?"

"Oh, and here I thought you guys just looked forward to messing with MI6." Jonas laughed good-naturedly.

Markus sniffed the air. "I smell food."

"Yeah, spaghetti," Lachlan replied. "Yours is on the counter."

He headed into the kitchen, and, within a matter of moments, they heard the microwave turning on.

Lachlan walked in and sat down beside him. "Any idea what's going on?"

"No more than anyone else," Markus noted. "It's a shit show for sure."

"I just don't understand why."

"Unless they're after her."

Lachlan smiled, rubbing the back of his neck. "That's the conclusion I came to," he replied. "Nothing else makes sense. For any of the rest of us, they would have just taken out all the vehicles," he noted. "But they didn't, so they must have wanted somebody alive, and the only life they would care about enough would be hers."

"That's the conclusion I came to as well," Markus agreed.

"She's really resistant to the idea," Lachlan added.

"Of course she is. Nobody wants to think they are the target. Nobody wants to think that all of this is about her."

"So, is it related to the banking case, or is it something more personal?" Lachlan asked Markus.

Markus turned toward him. "I assumed it was the banking case."

"It crossed my mind that it could be personal, but I know that Tesla has already done a full check on her and hasn't come up with anything in the personal realm."

"No, but you also know that relationship shit like that can hang around for a very long time."

"Too damn long," Lachlan replied. "Just when you think you're getting away from that stuff, it comes around and bites you in the ass. It's so much better if all our enemies end up dead." At that, Lachlan burst out laughing.

Markus grinned at him. "Too bad we can't see that happening anytime soon."

"Nope, the bad guys keep getting away one way or another, at least when any of them are alive," Lachlan added. "I have to admit it makes our life easier when they don't survive, although I know it's not what the brass likes to see."

"I think the brass likes it just fine," Markus replied, with an eye roll. "They just don't want to be *seen* liking it."

"Yeah, and, when these guys are arrested, it seems like they get off way too easy. Or get people killed until their cases are miraculously dismissed."

"That's why we just keep doing what we're assigned to do," Markus stated, with a smile.

"So how are you doing these days?"

"I'm doing good."

"Did you ever consider this might be related to you?" Lachlan asked his buddy.

"I hope not," Markus admitted, "but I've been on just as many missions as you, I guess, but with some differences."

"What differences?" Lachlan asked.

"Nothing major, but it's still the same deal. When the

ship is going down, you know they tend to look at us to see how far that ship is sinking."

"Right. I never quite understood that philosophy," Lachlan stated, with a grin.

"Nothing to understand really, they're just always looking for somebody to blame."

"So you don't think this is related to your history?" Lachlan asked.

"No, I don't."

Markus asked Lachlan, "Do you?"

"No, I don't think so."

Markus nodded. "I spent a lot of time out there, thinking hard and trying to figure out who and what it could be, but honestly? ... Nothing's really coming to mind."

"So, we're back to her then," Lachlan stated.

"Unless it's Jonas."

"No kidding." Lachlan began speaking a little louder, with a nod toward the other room. "Jesus, I can't even get my head around how many people would want to take out Jonas."

From the other room, Jonas called out, "I heard that."

"*Whoops!*" Lachlan called back, as they all enjoyed a chuckle.

Jonas came into the kitchen and joined them. "I think it's got to be the banking angle," he suggested.

"That does make the most sense, even though Leah doesn't really want to see it," Lachlan agreed. "The rest of us are pretty well in agreement, thinking she is the target."

"So, what do they stand to get out of kidnapping her? That's the real question. I mean, are they assuming that, without the analyst, the government would be paralyzed? Stupid assumption, but they may not know that."

"And that's probably why that theory won't fly," Markus noted.

"But the other thing would be the possibility that they're trying to find out what she might know."

"Which would suck," Lachlan stated. "Because, if she knows anything, of course it goes to the government level."

"Exactly."

Just then Lachlan's phone buzzed, and he looked down to find a message from Mason. He looked at the guys and said, "Mason wants an update."

"Yeah, I told him that I would give him one when I got in," Markus shared. "Give me a minute. I'll go talk to him." He got up and walked out of the room.

Lachlan looked over at Jonas and quipped, "See? If you weren't here, we'd be having that call on Speakerphone."

Jonas glared at him. "I wouldn't say that I have any problem with Mason."

"Maybe not, but you know there's only so much information we can share without having you get us into deep shit for it."

At that, Jonas shrugged. "That is entirely your problem. And don't worry. I've got plenty shit of my own to deal with. No shortage of which involves you guys or your counterparts in other organizations, by the way."

"I'm sure you do," Lachlan agreed. "But the problem we share now is that we still have to solve this thing. The trouble is, it's distracting us from focusing on the next bank hit." At that, he froze and looked at Jonas. "Jesus, could it be that simple? It's been right there in front of us the whole time. Maybe that's the reason behind the attack." Lachlan stared slowly at the guy.

At that, Jonas turned and looked at him. "You think so?"

"We're looking for a reason, and the hits definitely qualify. It has completely shifted our focus," Lachlan stated, "and that's not a good thing."

Jonas frowned at that. "It's so tempting to go wake her up."

"Don't bother," Lachlan replied. "From what I understand, almost all analysts are hard sleepers. She'll be dead to the world with that powerful brain of hers. And, until she wakes up and is ready to function again, you won't get anything useful out of her."

He nodded. "I wouldn't do it anyway. I'm sure it's much better to give her a chance to rest and to recuperate."

"I did check on her, and she is sound asleep," Lachlan noted.

"She's stressed and obviously not used to dealing with attacks like this," Jonas replied.

"Neither are you," Lachlan stated, looking over at him. "At least not in such a personal sense. How are you holding up?"

"I'm fine." Jonas gave him a wave of his hand. "And, no, I'm not used to it, not anymore. Most of the time I'm working closer to home these days. We haven't had anything like this in quite a while. Though, at the same time, it would be nice to know that she's doing okay."

Lachlan turned and looked in the direction of the bedrooms. "Yeah, I can go and check on her in a bit."

Jonas looked at him, then grinned and said, "Or I could."

Lachlan glared at him. "So, this is now personal, is it?"

"She's a beautiful lady," Jonas stated.

"And here I thought you were taken."

"Nope, we broke up a while ago," he shared. "It's a very

strange affair."

"Sounds like it." Lachlan stared at him. "And I can't say I like the idea of you making a move on her."

"Not making a move at all," Jonas argued, "but that doesn't mean I'm blind to having a beautiful woman around."

"Maybe you should just keep your hands to yourself."

"Or what?" Jonas asked, with a big grin. "Is this all about you and your client?"

"I don't have a client," Lachlan replied. But inside, he knew how much he didn't want Jonas to move in that direction. Lachlan shrugged.

Jonas added, "Personally I don't think she's likely to have time for either one of us. She's all business."

"Sure she is, … for the moment, and then she will be again, until something else comes along." Lachlan laughed. "People like that, it's just how they are. In the meantime though, it's nice to have her around, but I sure wouldn't be pushing it."

"Of course not," Jonas sated, "but I can be nice, can't I?"

"Sure you can. As a matter of fact, it's like a job requirement, you know? … We have to be nice to the analyst," he teased. "Just keep it under control."

"And I'm back to that *or else* thing," Jonas noted. "You think I haven't seen how you look at her?"

"Oh hell no," Lachlan snapped. "I'm not going there with you."

"You already went there," he stated, with a grin. "I saw the look on your face when I said I might go wake her up."

He shrugged. "Just a little protective, that's all."

"You keep telling yourself that," Jonas replied. "Maybe you'll even eventually believe it."

And, with that, Lachlan got up. "Regardless of all that's going on in that conversation, I'll grab a power nap."

"I know you don't want me to, but I'll volunteer anyway. So, if you need somebody to stand guard," Jonas suggested, "I'm available."

"Just wake me up soon."

Without a backward glance Lachlan headed to his room.

CHAPTER 4

L EAH WOKE UP startled and bolted out of bed. She turned and looked around in shock.

Where the hell was she?

She didn't recognize her surroundings. And then it hit her hard, and she remembered what had happened. The chase in the car, ending up at the safe house.

Here she was with strangers in a strange apartment. Sometimes life sucked.

She shook her head at that, then reached up and scrubbed her face. She checked her phone and saw that it was 6:15 a.m. That was not necessarily too early for her, but she suspected the men would be up already, definitely Lachlan, and potentially Axel as well.

She walked into the bathroom, decided to take a shower to get herself fully awake, so she could catch up on the work she had to do. Turning on the hot water, she waited until the heat came through the faucet and stepped in. When she was done, she grabbed a towel and scrubbed down, glaring at yesterday's clothing, which was all she had to wear.

She had no choice but to wear the same old clothes. She brushed her teeth with an unopened new toothbrush she found here, then towel-dried her hair and headed to the kitchen. As she walked in, she nodded. "I figured you would be up."

"Up and at 'em," Lachlan replied, getting up. He walked toward her, looking her over. "How are you doing?"

She looked up at him. "I'd be better if I had clean clothes, but other than that"—she shrugged—"I slept like a baby, so that's all good." She spied the coffeepot, and her face lit up. "Oh, yay, coffee. Thank goodness." She walked over, poured herself a cup.

"Do you live on the stuff too?" he asked.

She chuckled. "Don't we all?" she murmured.

"It's funny," he began, "because I had a friend I used to work with, and he didn't drink tea or coffee. Can you believe it?" He stared at her with an incredulous expression.

She nodded. "I know. Some people …" She shook her head.

"Right? It made me very distrustful of him for the longest time."

She looked over at him. "Just absolutely no reason to avoid coffee, in my opinion."

"That's the way it is though."

"It is an odd thing, isn't it? I wonder what they do instead? It's kind of a social thing, you know, to just have a drink in the morning. You get up and enjoy a cup of coffee as part of your routine. So, if you don't do that, what do you do?"

"In his case, he'd get up and go to his laptop instead. It's what we all do anyway," he noted, "but the coffee just makes it go down that much easier."

Coffee in hand, Leah sat down at the table. "Did we get groceries?"

"Our delivery is supposed to be here at eight," he noted, checking his watch.

"Ah, so we're waiting for food then, are we?"

"Unless you want leftover spaghetti." He pointed to the plate that somebody had already used.

"Did you have spaghetti this morning?" she asked, smiling.

"I had a little bit an hour or so ago," he admitted. "I'll wait now for the other food."

"Right." She decided spaghetti for breakfast wasn't her thing. "No, I'll be fine. I just want coffee for now, and then I'll get something, whenever we get the food delivery." She looked around. "What about Markus?"

"He's back out again. We all switched out during the night."

"Nobody watching this place?"

"Nobody that we saw anyway," he stated cautiously.

At his phrase, she turned and shot him a sharp look. "So, you're worried about someone we can't see?"

He nodded. "Yes. There is just that much more of an opportunity for people to track us if they know the area we disappeared into."

"Right," she murmured. She shook her head. "I also need to check my email."

"You can do that now, with your coffee," he replied. "I'll bring you a laptop to use." He stood and left the room, soon bringing one over to her.

She opened it up and nodded. "So nobody has been on it?"

"Nope, it's all yours," he confirmed. "Nobody wants to make you feel like you can't be trusted, or, you know, like we're using the same equipment."

"I don't know what to think," she admitted. "My mind went in a million different directions overnight. Since I woke up, I keep thinking somebody knows about us."

"So the questions then are," he began, "how much do they know, and what is known? It could have been just an innocent comment in passing, asking what your schedule was like or if you would be in the office tomorrow or something like that."

"I'm thinking that's probably what it was," she replied.

"All my people are well paid. The last time I did a check, I saw absolutely no sign of financial hardship with any of them."

"And no family issues?"

"No."

"But that can change in a heartbeat too," he murmured.

She nodded. "Absolutely," she agreed, even though she hated to. When she heard an odd buzz, she turned and looked at him in surprise, feeling everything inside her freezing up again.

He nodded at her and smiled. "It's okay. It's probably just Axel."

At that, she spun around looking for him. "I didn't realize he wasn't here."

"He went to get food."

"Ah, the eight a.m. delivery." She checked the time on the wall clock. "But he's early."

"He is, and that's okay too."

Leah smiled. "I could eat. How about you?"

He nodded, standing up. "Yep. As long as it's him at the door."

She frowned when he didn't go anywhere.

"And that's the reason for me standing here right now," he explained. "If it's Axel, he'll buzz again in another minute, with an interesting pattern."

Almost immediately the doorbell buzzed again, as if

sending out the first few refrains of a song.

She frowned at that. "I don't know how he did that," she stated cautiously, "but I presume that's him then."

"Yeah, absolutely."

"And you still won't let him in?" she asked.

"Nope," he said, "Jonas already has."

"Ah," she murmured. "I forgot he was here again."

At that, Jonas appeared at the kitchen entryway, a smile on his face. "Don't worry. I'm trying hard not to take that personally."

She smiled at him. "And you shouldn't take it personally. I'm still not fully awake."

"I got it," he replied. "I just prefer to think that I'm a little more memorable than that."

She chuckled. "Everything here and now is memorable," she noted, laughing inwardly. "But I'm not sure you really want to be included in that category."

"Maybe not," he admitted. "However, we do have Axel here."

And, with that, Axel made his way into the kitchen carrying multiple bags.

She hopped up and walked over. "Can I give you a hand with that?"

"I would have had a hand with it," Axel joked, "if Jonas would have helped. Unlike you, he seemed to be totally okay with just opening the door for me."

She shot Jonas a look and a frown, and he raised both hands. "Hey, Axel didn't say he needed help, so it didn't occur to me to offer."

She rolled her eyes at that. "Amazing," she murmured. "I would have thought you would have been more intuitive than that. Someone with their hands full, who took the time, effort, and risk to go for supplies? It seems the least one could do is lend a hand, … without specifically being asked. Common courtesy and all."

"Nope," Jonas argued, "never occurred to me." And he spoke with such cheerful sincerity in his voice that it was hard to take issue with him.

She had never really met anybody like him, and even now it was hard to argue with the whole positive-thinking jolly-good-cheer thing he had going for him. As soon as the bags were set on the table, she started digging through them.

"As you're unloading that," Axel noted, "remember a bunch of us need food, and we need to get to it fairly quickly. So set out anything that looks promising."

"Got it," she replied. "I can cook a little but not tons."

"I do have a little bit of ready-made stuff in there as well," Axel mentioned.

"I'm totally okay to do a bit of cooking," she replied. "I'll just need some help with portions and things."

During that exchange, Lachlan had reached into the bags and pulled out bacon and eggs. "I'll have these on in no time."

"Good. Make sure lots of toast goes with it too, would you?" Axel stated, with a yawn.

"Long night?" she asked, as she quietly studied his face.

"Sure was," he stated, with a shrug. "Aren't they all?"

"Sorry to admit it, but I slept my fill," she said on a wince. "So, in my case, … not so much."

"Good for you," Lachlan stated. "We'll need your brain-power today, so let's hope it got recharged overnight."

At that, she barely withheld a grimace because, while they definitely needed her analytic skills, and somewhat desperately at that, she wasn't entirely certain that she had anything to offer. This case was too wide open and seemed to be going in directions that she didn't really want to pursue.

She already knew that all of them were analyzing her team, and that just made her feel worse. If it turned out that she'd had anything to do with the people who were involved in this nightmare, then that would be on her. Even though most people would say that she couldn't take that on and that she'd have no reason to feel guilty about it, she still would. They were her team and, therefore, her responsibility.

By the time she had the groceries put away, the happy smell of sizzling bacon filled the air. She walked over to Lachlan and asked, "Anything I can do?"

He nodded. "Sure, you can make toast."

And, with that, she grabbed the closest loaf of bread and started popping pieces into the toaster. "Any idea how many we'll need?" she asked, after she filled the toaster with four slices and hesitated.

He looked at the toaster and said, "At least two per person."

She shrugged. "That's a lot of toast," she murmured.

"We're feeding a lot of mouths too," he reminded her.

It was hard to argue with that logic, but she started the toaster, then found the butter in the fridge that she had just put away. She brought it out and set it on the counter, then went to the cupboard for plates. As she watched, Lachlan now cracked eggs into a bowl.

"I noticed you didn't ask if there's a particular way that people want their food cooked," she murmured, with a grin.

"Nope, no time for that special-order stuff. If we were at home and if it were a barbecue or something, I could ask how you wanted your steak. However, right now, given the circumstances, we'll cook some food, and people will eat it, or they won't," he stated, like a simple fact. "In a place and a situation like this, the leftovers won't last long enough for anybody to argue about."

And that explained why he was scrambling what must be about eighteen eggs. As he now studied the rest of the eggs in the carton, she asked, "Do we really need more than that?"

"That's the question, isn't it?" he noted, frowning. "My instincts tell me to go for it and to use them all."

She stared at him in shock and then shrugged. "Then listen to your instincts, I would say. I am hungry, though I can't imagine I've ever eaten more than two scrambled eggs at a meal," she murmured.

"That's the thing though. In situations like this, not only do you get extra famished but it's much harder to fill that hunger." He went on, adding simply, "Nerves will do it, especially in any kind of panicking situation. All kinds of reactions are triggered, but, at the moment, it'll be more about filling the physical needs than the emotional."

She wasn't exactly sure what he was trying to say, but she was willing to go along. By the time he started serving food onto plates, everybody already sat at the dining room table, nursing their coffee and discussing the case. She wished she had something to offer, but she didn't.

Just then, Jonas turned and looked at her. "Do you have any updates?"

She shook her head. "No. I have to talk to Tesla and see how she did overnight."

"Wouldn't she have contacted you already?"

"Yes, I would have thought so," she replied, "so I'll assume she hasn't found anything. Unless we have communication issues again with the net. But since everybody else seems to talk back and forth, I'll presume the former. I'll definitely be checking in, right after breakfast." He just nodded and didn't say any more. Looking at him, she asked, "What about your office? Anything?"

"Nothing yet," Jonas confirmed.

"*Great,*" she replied, "so we have a whole lot of nothing."

"That's just the way some of these cases go," Axel noted. "Yet it won't stay that way. Something will break it wide open, and then you'll be wishing you had more time to breathe."

She nodded. "I get that. I really do. But I can't help but wish that something would break already, so we can figure it out and be done with it."

"Well, it won't happen that way," Lachlan stated, with a grin. "Life is never quite so accommodating."

"Why not?" she asked in exasperation. "Surely these guys can't keep up this crap."

"The question is why they're doing it in the first place, and, if it's just about money, then how much do they actually have to have before it becomes enough?"

"People like this, … do they ever have enough?" she asked. "I would assume they'd keep going as long as they could, until they were caught. But then, if you think about it, that's a stupid way to do business because, once you've got a certain amount of money, everybody could get their split and take off, never to be heard from again."

"Or, as we've seen time and time again," Axel added slowly, "someone decides *not* to split it. Then, all of a sudden, we have bodies showing up that we weren't expecting."

"You mean, a falling out among thieves?" she asked curiously.

"Exactly," Axel stated. "Once people start to look at how far the money would go or not go, or the risk of people knowing what they know, everybody starts rethinking their plans. This is where it can get quite dangerous. It also depends on how many are involved and how many were intended to be involved at the end of the day."

"Meaning, how many would ever get a payout," Lachlan had to clarify, looking at the confusion on Leah's face.

Axel nodded. "All too often, people who thought they would be part of the end result get a reality check somewhere along the line."

LACHLAN WATCHED THE uncertainty cross her face, as she thought about what was going on, even as she ate her breakfast. It was easy to read her face. So much so that there was no way she could successfully play poker because her every thought was visible on that very mobile gaze.

It was interesting to watch because Lachlan wasn't used to having anybody around who was so open. It was also surprising given her work. When she caught him looking, she frowned at him, and he frowned back. She rolled her eyes as if to say he was being childish, and he was, but, at the same time, it kept the air light and her mood a little bit sunnier than might be expected right now.

As soon as they were done eating, he hopped up and offered, "I'll do the dishes. You go get started on your work."

She nodded. "I feel like I'm a slacker now, hanging out with you guys."

"It's not a case of being a slacker. It's a matter of getting that rejuvenation so that you can continue," he explained. "Just because we can work through the night doesn't mean we work effectively."

"We can do it for a while," Axel interjected, "but, at some point in time, everybody has to recharge. You needed recharging."

"Yeah, but now you're expecting great things."

He chuckled. "Yeah, we sure are. Mostly because you're our only hope."

"And that's not true," she argued. "What really pisses me off is I could use my team's help to do something about this other bank."

"If you give us the names of the important people at the target bank, we can start checking to make sure that everybody is fine."

"I was hoping that would have already been done," she replied. "I left instructions for it to be done, but that was yesterday, before all this blew up."

"That's fine," Lachlan replied. "Check on it now, and, if it's not done, we can take care of it."

She nodded, then grabbed her laptop and headed off to the living room for some uninterrupted work.

While Lachlan finished up the dishes, Axel went for a nap, and Markus was already out on guard duty. That left Jonas. Typically he just sat here, an odd look on his face.

"What's up?" Lachlan asked him.

"Just this whole scenario," Jonas replied. "I keep waiting for a second attack."

"I was wondering that myself," he agreed, "but so far nobody has made a move on us, and that can't be because they can't find us. The minute everybody starts going in and out, you know that our safety perimeter dwindles, and yet we have to eat."

"Yes, and they would be counting on that," Jonas responded immediately. "What would you like to do?"

"Personally I'd like to leave," he stated calmly. "But I'm not sure that's the best thing for me to do at this point."

"For you or for the case?"

"Both. I'm really hoping that Leah will come up with something." Lachlan paused. "I think she already has, and, if she left instructions for that work to be carried out, yet it wasn't, I'll be looking very closely at the people who were told to carry it out."

"Ah," Jonas replied, with a small nod, "good point."

"Did you ever get the name of the bank that she thought was next?"

"No, because, as far as the intel goes, it didn't match up."

"Yet did MI6 ask her how she got that information? Or why she came to that conclusion against everybody else's input?"

"I don't think we've given her much time to double-check her theory on the next target," Jonas replied. "Now that she's back up and mentally solid again, let's hope that she's got some answers."

She walked in at that point in time, reaching for the coffee. She turned and looked at Jonas. "I do have some answers. None of the work I left to be done was completed. Now I need to have a talk with that person."

"Who was it? Someone you suspect?"

"Not at all. Under normal circumstances, it would have been done immediately, come hell or high water," she murmured. "The fact that it's not been completed just terrifies me."

"So you're thinking that something has happened?"

She nodded slowly. "I don't know that, of course, but

it's definitely a concern. We need to find her."

"What's her name?" Lachlan asked. When Leah hesitated, Lachlan laid down the law to her. "We're a team here, Leah. Either you are working with us or against us." He held up a hand to stop her from arguing with him. "I know you're trying to protect your team, but that is where you're wrong. You are prejudging, where your mind must be open to all alternatives. Surely you realize that someone you trust can be bought, can be threatened, can be blackmailed?"

Leah pinched her lips together.

"What's her name?" Lachlan demanded.

She sighed and gave in. "Pamela. Pamela Betts."

Jonas asked, "What about your boss? Does he know?"

"Yeah, I've shared this with him already, but, just in case, I have the list of names here of those who overheard me giving this particular job to Pamela, along with the bank that I thought would be hit next."

"Do you think Betts was pulled off the case?"

"That was my first thought, which is why I tried to contact her at home on her landline and got no answer. Pamela's not responding to her cell either."

"And you think something has happened?"

"I don't know." She hesitated. "What I can tell you is that I left explicit instructions for something to be done. And, while it wasn't a popular move, and the rest of the group thought it was a waste of man-hours, I still needed to get it off my list. And since Pamela is not responding in any way, it could mean a few different things. It could be that they've been ordered not to," she explained, "or they could have chosen to ignore it, in which case I've misread some things. Either way, that makes me very, very unhappy, but that's not necessarily anybody else's concern at this point."

"Right," Lachlan replied. "So we'll get right on that." He smiled at her, his hand out. "You can't protect your team if they did something wrong. So I need a copy of those explicit instructions."

"I need a copy too," Jonas added.

She sighed and turned to go to her bedroom. After a moment, she returned with a printed list and placed it in Lachlan's hand.

He handed Jonas the duplicate copy of the information, as he studied the names of the primary banking officers in her target bank. "It's not as big of a bank as I was expecting."

"I know," she agreed. "All I can tell you is that every set of data that I ran … pointed to this one."

"Do you have a theory on why they didn't believe you then?"

"Because it's a smaller bank than the others hit, and every bank the hackers have hit so far is huge."

Lachlan nodded. "And, of course, they don't like anomalies."

"Nope, they don't," she agreed. "And all I can do is tell them what I find."

"And be pissed off when they don't follow through of course."

"Wouldn't you be pissed off too?" she challenged.

"Of course," he stated. "Nothing quite like having people ask you for information in your specific area of expertise, only to have your information pushed out of the way as being inaccurate."

"Exactly." She nodded. "And they can say what they want, but, as far as I'm concerned, it's still our best chance of finding these guys."

"And you're thinking it'll be the next job or possibly the

one after that?"

She stopped, frowned at him, and asked, "Why would you say that?"

"Because of the fact that it's a smaller bank, so I'm not sure that they have pulled enough money yet."

She looked at him and, with her voice distant, added, "So you don't think it's a likely target either?"

"No," he argued, "not at all. I'm asking because, if this is the job that's next, we have to really consider what their motive is."

"Why would you say that?" she asked.

"Because then you have to wonder if they haven't been planning to target somebody in particular at this bank all along," Jonas interjected, stepping in to assist Lachlan. "And it has nothing to do with money. That's just a side benefit."

CHAPTER 5

WITH THEIR THOUGHTS ringing in her ears, Leah returned to the computer room and went over her data once again, then sent a text message to Lachlan, telling him that she had rerun the data and that it still came up the same.

He walked into the computer room, where she was working. "I wasn't doubting you. I'm just trying to figure out what these hackers and the kidnappers are doing and why."

"What you say makes sense," she agreed, "but the rest of this sure doesn't."

"It does and it doesn't," he murmured. "But, the fact of the matter is, if this is the way it is, then we have to figure it out, and we have to do it fast. Because something here doesn't seem to fit properly, and we don't have time for mistakes."

"I get that," she replied. "I really do. It's just frustrating because this is what I'm supposed to do, and then, when I give people the information, they don't want to use it."

"And what about the staff member you mentioned earlier. Pamela Betts?"

"I still can't get ahold of her," Leah murmured. "I contacted my boss again."

"What did he say?"

"He says he'll continue to try to find her. Sent a team over to her residence, as far as I know."

"Okay, good enough," Lachlan noted. "Let's hope that it's nothing."

"Maybe." Leah looked over at him. "Ever have that feeling that makes your gut turn and twist?"

He nodded. "Is that what you're feeling?"

She nodded slowly. "I know it should be nothing, but it doesn't feel like nothing at all. It feels like a big ugly pile of something."

"I hope not," he replied, "because that could be pretty serious. As in fatal."

At that, she stared at him. "And to think I was thinking about betrayal, not death," she murmured.

"I don't know what I'm thinking," he added instantly. "I just know that *Houston, we have a problem* and that we need to figure it out."

She smiled at the lighthearted comment. "You guys are really good at handling all these stressful scenarios with humor, aren't you?"

"It's what we do," he stated. "I gather you haven't dealt with cases like this very much."

"No," she murmured. "Can't say I want to do too many more of them either."

He chuckled. "If and when that ever becomes an option, let me know."

At that, she stared at him. "Meaning that you think this kind of work is commonplace?"

"Oh, it is. Absolutely it is," he declared, with a smile. "Trying to figure out what people are up to—terrorists, killers, governments—it's all about getting into the minds of the perpetrators, like with law enforcement profilers, but we often use analysts."

"Yeah?" she asked. "This is a new department for me."

"You can't take these criminal matters to heart," he reminded her. "An awful lot of crappy things are happening out in the world that we don't have too much control over. At one point in time you'll find that it will take the stuffing right out of you if you let yourself get sucked into everything."

"I think it's a case of too-late-already," she murmured.

He nodded gently. "Yeah, I wouldn't be at all surprised, not with your first-time handling something like this," he added. "But just go easy on yourself right now and remember that there's no such thing as making a mistake but of gaining experience. All we can do is go by the data and see what it brings us." At that, he turned and walked out.

It seemed to her to be a far cry from what he'd said this morning, but maybe not. Maybe she'd just been super sensitive and hadn't understood what he was trying to say. And it was true in the sense that this wasn't her normal thing. She was an analyst and certainly didn't go out in the field doing this kind of US Navy SEAL stuff.

She was also new here in this location, with this staff of hers. Still getting established. Still getting her feet under her. Still being tested in a way. Hard to not feel like she was failing. It was hard to stay detached from the emotional side and from the stress. Information, data points, entering new bits and pieces, and analyzing it all as it came up allowed her to keep a little more distance from all this, theoretically anyway.

Doing this right now from a safe house, after the harrowing escape from being followed and shot at yesterday, didn't provide that same buffer zone. And it was definitely affecting her, she admitted to herself, though she didn't really want to see it. Having her requests and recommendations dismissed by her coworkers or bosses had stung and had underlined her already flaring insecurities.

And that was foolish. She was here, just gathering and analyzing information, and, if they didn't want to listen to her findings, what was it to her? Except that she was convinced that they were wrong. She was right about the bank to be targeted next, and that drove her wild with frustration. What if somebody else died?

Her information was something that they could use to help, even to prevent, but instead nobody gave a crap. And the fact that nobody gave a crap is where she got hung up. Surely there was more to life than dealing with people who just heard their own ideas and weren't interested in listening to hers.

She knew that Tesla would tell her that they just didn't know Leah well enough yet and hadn't had long enough to actually understand that Leah knew what she was doing and that she was very good at her job. The trouble was, Leah didn't necessarily know how to tell anybody that either. She was feeling hamstrung by her superiors, though she knew that wasn't anything new to these guys, not with their various military backgrounds.

It was just frustrating and was the first time she'd ever really come up against it, at least to this degree. Just then her phone rang. It was her boss.

"Hey, there's no sign of her."

"What?"

"Betts didn't show up for work."

"What?"

"She didn't log into the building at all. Her security code

has not been detected, and, according to the doorman at her apartment, she didn't come home last night."

"Crap," Leah replied. "Do you know when she logged out of the building?"

"She left at nine forty-two p.m."

"Which is suspiciously late."

"It is, indeed," her boss noted. "We've sent a team to look for her and to search her apartment and any parking related to that, and we've requested the video feeds of her apartment, but so far I haven't received them."

"Good enough," she murmured. "Please let me know when you find her."

"What information did you give her?"

As much as Leah hated to, she explained about pulling all the names and locations of everybody who worked for the bank which Leah had identified as the likely next target.

"Even though everybody decided you were wrong?" he asked.

"Yes," she stated. "Just because you think I'm wrong doesn't mean I am. And we needed that information anyway in order to prove whether I was right or wrong and to move on."

"Right," he noted. "But that information wasn't terribly important."

"I don't know about that," she argued. "I would think it definitely was, particularly right now, after the attack on us and Pamela missing too."

"Maybe," he murmured. "I'm not exactly sure what's going on."

"No, and that's one of the reasons why I wanted this checked," she murmured. "We have to at least knock it off the board as a possibility."

"Fine," he replied. "I'll get somebody else on it."

"And fast, please," she added, before he could hang up. Of course she knew that her last little comment was not likely to go down too well. But she was the one stuck in a safe house, waiting, and the fact that information she'd requested was so slow in coming wasn't helping.

At that, she put down her phone and rubbed her forehead, only to have Lachlan look at her expectantly.

"No luck?"

"They can't find her," she explained. "She left work at nine forty-two last night to go home. There's no sign of her entering her apartment building yesterday, according to the night doorman. The video camera feeds have been requested, but my boss didn't have copies of them yet."

He looked at her steadily for a moment. "Do you think it's pertinent?"

"Yes, it's pertinent," she snapped. "Why?"

He smiled at her and nodded. "Is there a reason why you're waiting for your boss to get that video footage?"

She stared at him, frowning. "Yeah, that's what we do—normally." She hesitated. "But you're right. Today is not a normal day, and this is not a normal scenario. Shit ..."

"You have a choice."

"Between my gut instincts and too much government influence?" She shook her head.

"Between too much right and too much wrong," he noted. "Not necessarily too much right from the people you needed it from."

"It's all about bureaucracy in this instance," she noted in frustration. "And I don't even know at what point in time I'm allowed to break the rules."

"If you lose your job over this point, how would you feel

about it?"

"At this point, I'm frustrated," she stated. "So if I lose my job, I lose it."

"And if you break the rules but save a life in the process?"

"Then I'd be happy to break the rules constantly," she replied.

"Got it," he murmured, smiling as she slammed away at her keyboard. "So what will you do?"

"I'm already doing it," she snapped. "Go away and leave me alone."

He laughed. "I'd rather stick close."

"Then you'll just be a distraction," she murmured.

"A big one?" he asked, curiosity in his voice.

She lifted her head and turned from the keyboard and glared at him. "Seriously? You want to discuss this now?"

"Sure, why not?" he asked. "Life is for the living, and you've got to remember to live."

"Right now," she explained, "I'm trying to save some people who quite likely won't make it through tomorrow."

"Are you that sure about that?"

She nodded. "Yes, which is why I was trying to get the damn information to begin with."

"Okay," he said, "I'll get it for you."

"My boss is supposedly giving that job to somebody else now."

Lachlan waved a hand. "That's BS, and you know it. I'll do it."

"Okay." She didn't really know what to say to that, but he was already seated beside her with a laptop. By the time she had the video feed at work up and running, Lachlan was talking to Axel and splitting up the list to call and ensure that every one of these people on Leah's list, who could be in danger, were accounted for.

Meanwhile Leah spent time going through the video feed from the previous day, her attention focused on Betts—the coworker and friend Leah had given the work request to—as she got into an elevator to her apartment the video was working but when she was about to get off, the video feed encountered a glitch.

Leah swore because, when it came back on again, she saw no sign of her friend. She watched through the whole night of footage but found nothing, found no sign of Pamela. "The computers went out and the elevator was stuck for almost five minutes starting at nine forty-five p.m.," she relayed to Lachlan.

"That's the right timing."

"It certainly is," she murmured, "and a time gap of four minutes and thirty-six seconds is in this glitch. So she could have gone to another floor or even to the ladies' room and maybe returned to her office, like if she forgot something, then left again, but we just don't know because we don't see her again after that glitch."

"So, we have no idea if she is missing voluntarily or was picked up? How do you feel about your gut instincts now?"

"Shitty." She glared at him. "Shittier than I already did, so thanks for that."

He nodded. "You're welcome. Information is power, and now we know that there's a problem. She was quite possibly either kidnapped or—"

"Or she's in on it. Yes, I got that." She scrubbed at her face. "Did anybody track down the employees of my proposed target bank yet?"

"We've got a team on it." When his phone buzzed, he

checked the Caller ID on his screen. "Oh, that's Tesla." He nodded at Leah. "Yeah, what's up?" he asked Tesla. Leah watched him as he stared at her steadily. "Yes, I know. Leah's just hacked into the video cameras in the building where she and Pamela Betts work, and somebody is playing games." Then he quickly explained what happened. "No, I hear you. We've got most of the names on our parts of the list already accounted for."

Leah tapped Lachlan on his knee urgently. "Did Tesla get through the ones I gave her?"

He nodded to Leah. "Yeah, got it," he told Tesla. "Thanks, we'll talk later." And, with that call disconnected, he shared with Leah, "All the names that Tesla has run so far are clear."

Leah winced at that. "Of course they are," she muttered. "Everybody will just think I'm nuts."

At that, he smiled at her and shook his head. "Hey, Tesla doesn't think you're nuts. She ran the data, and she happens to agree with your conclusion on that target bank."

She beamed at him. "Yay for something," she muttered, "and, of course, now that Tesla says it's important, I'm sure there'll be action."

He smiled. "Would you rather be right, or would you rather save lives?" She glared at him, and he nodded. "It often ends up being just that simple."

She raised both hands. "Fine. I don't care about being right. This whole scenario is just bad news."

"And I get that," he agreed. "So let's get the rest of these names sorted and see what we can come up with."

Then, in a surprise move, Axel popped into the computer room with a big grin on his face. "We got something."

Lachlan exhaled. *About damn time.*

LACHLAN SLIPPED INTO the unmarked car parked several blocks from the safe house. Now that some physical action was happening, he felt better. Nothing worse than sitting around twiddling your thumbs, waiting for information to come in. Sure, everybody needed a chance to rest and to regroup. Yet, at the same time, too much was going on with the bad guys, and Lachlan didn't like being pinned down.

He pulled into traffic and drove toward Betts's apartment building. He would do a quick recon on the missing woman's apartment to see if he could come up with anything. Then he would swing past several of these other addresses to make sure nothing had happened to these other people in Leah's team.

Another team from her office and yet another team from Jonas's office would be reporting in as well. Everybody had balked at that, but Jonas had refused to be kept out. And he had the clout to get that too. Just too much going on, and now that an analyst assistant from Leah's office was missing, the stakes were even higher. While Lachlan and Jonas may not completely trust each other, this was a matter of saving lives, and they would never play around with that. Another problem was that nobody completely trusted anybody else in these matters, and that would make it difficult going forward.

As Lachlan neared the general area of Pamela Betts's apartment building, he pulled off into an alleyway several blocks away, then slowly walked his way on the street toward the apartment. He studied the surrounding area and found it to be fairly residential, with easy access to public transportation—almost within walking distance, if somebody was of the mind to do so.

As he reached the apartment building, an elderly woman was coming out, so he held the door for her and slipped in behind her. It always bothered him when access was that easy because it meant that everybody in the building was pretty lazy about security. And any physical security guard for the front door was not here at the moment. Granted, everybody deserved bathroom breaks and lunch, but that's why two people should be on duty at all times. Even so, internal cameras should have been installed too. None were in the lobby. That meant none were elsewhere. Lachlan shook his head.

In theory these security measures here at Betts's apartment building may have sounded just fine, especially to the owner with a tight fist on his wallet, and that was great, only as long as there were no problems. However, the minute there was a problem, it became a huge issue. And, right now, as far as Lachlan was concerned, this was a huge issue. He raced up the stairs to the fourth floor, and he checked all the apartments on that side.

There wasn't any sign of life in any of the other apartments. He presumed most people were at work for the day, but he had no way to know for sure.

When he saw nobody around, he tapped lightly on Betts's door. When he got no answer, he knocked again. Still no answer. Pulling the pick from his back pocket, he quickly unlocked the door and stepped inside, closing it immediately behind him.

"Anyone here?" he called out. "Hello. It's building maintenance."

Still no answer. A weird emptiness hung around the place. He quickly moved through the living room, which just had a chair and a couch, with no personal effects. No pictures were on the wall, and nothing suggested anyone had actually enjoyed spending time here.

He frowned at that and moved quickly to the bedroom. If ever a place would reveal something about its occupant, it would usually be the bedroom. As he stepped through, he looked around the room. Suitcases on the bed made it apparent that somebody planned to make an exit soon.

The photos that he had expected to see up on the wall were sitting in a box, so Pamela had obviously been packing to leave, but was it to leave permanently or just to move to a different location? He quickly sent a text to Leah, asking if the woman was in the midst of a move.

Leah texted back immediately. **Not sure. She never mentioned it to me.**

That wasn't helpful at all because Lachlan had no way to determine whether Betts was moving to a different apartment or running from trouble. The bottom line was that he found no solid evidence of foul play, and that was not helpful either. Except for the fact that she wasn't here and apparently hadn't shown up at work at all today.

Which, in his book, revealed a lot.

He moved to the night tables beside the bed and noted they were empty. Everything had already been removed and tossed into a box. He searched under the bed and in the closet. She literally appeared to be within an hour of walking out of this property because everything not in suitcases sitting on her bed were in the boxes, all full, but not sealed or taped. Six boxes, two suitcases, and that was it.

He frowned at that and sent photos to Leah.

She called him almost immediately. "What's that?" she asked, puzzled.

"I was hoping you could tell me," he murmured. "This is

her bedroom."

"Seriously?" she gasped.

"Yeah, so I was hoping you had some idea of what was going on."

"I don't," she replied immediately. "But that doesn't look good, does it?"

"Not only does it not look good but she's not here, and that makes me even more worried."

"You think something happened to her?" she asked, her tone nervous.

"I can't rule it out, can you?"

"No, of course not. Damn it," she whispered. "What are the chances that somebody scared her, and she decided to book it?"

"So you tell me. What is she like?"

"On the nervous side," she stated immediately. "She didn't like it when we had to do work that she saw as dodgy."

"What do you mean by *dodgy*?"

"Looking into people's lives. She wasn't nosey. She often complained that she was in the wrong business, which is interesting since she stayed. Yet I had the sense that it was more a case of needing to work than wanting to do this work," she murmured.

"Ah, that kind of makes sense then, doesn't it?"

"Not really," she muttered. "None of this makes sense, and that's the part I continued to be confused by. There must be some answers, and the first thing I'd like to know," she added, her voice rising, "is where Pamela is and if she's okay."

"Do you think she left voluntarily?"

"Is her purse there?" she asked immediately.

He spun around. "Not here that I see. I'm heading into the kitchen. Maybe I'll find it there." As he went to the kitchen, he stopped and told Leah, "More boxes are here, as if she really was ready to pack up and leave."

"And that doesn't surprise me in a way. She might be just changing apartments. Let me contact my boss and see if he knows anything about it."

"Remember. He doesn't know I'm here," Lachlan cautioned her.

She froze and swore into the phone. "Damn it. I'm no good at this kind of stuff. If Ron had called me, I'd have told him immediately where you were."

He chuckled. "And you know, for a lot of people, it wouldn't make a damn bit of difference. However, in this case, we just don't know what's going on or who can be trusted, so it's better if we don't tell anybody much of anything."

"I get that. I really do," she murmured. "It's just that I'm not used to holding back info, so it feels off."

"See if you can find out from anybody at work—maybe under the guise of curiosity—if Betts was planning to move in with a boyfriend or to leave this job to do something else."

"Yeah, I can do something along those lines," she replied. "I'll get back to you."

And with that, she was gone, and Lachlan continued his search. The kitchen was all bare, including the fridge. He found the fresh food in a cooler, as if she were completely finished packing in here. Now he was even more worried about Betts. No sign of her purse yet.

He moved back to the bedroom and rechecked it. No sign of her purse and still no sign of a struggle. There was nothing suspicious here. But then, if somebody came at

Pamela with a gun, she may have gone quietly into the night, which was what most people did. They didn't raise a fuss, always hoping something would save them when they got outside, but often there was nothing to save them and nobody to rescue them.

Right now, all Lachlan saw was evidence of a woman who was busy packing and obviously quickly. Her clothes were just thrown into the suitcases; they weren't folded or carefully placed. Now a lot of people probably did pack that way, and he wouldn't be at all surprised if Pamela Betts were one of them. It's not as if Lachlan was the world's greatest packer either, but, stereotypical or not, he would have thought she would have taken a little more care.

In this case, he suspected that she just didn't have time to waste, and this was a *get in and get out* effort, as he looked around the desolate room.

"This might have been a good time to just grab your purse and run."

On that note, he resumed looking for a purse just in case she hadn't been snatched from work. He didn't see anything in the bedroom. Heading into the kitchen again, he checked all the usual places that somebody would likely toss a purse but found nothing.

However, when he opened up one of the drawers beside the fridge, a purse was jammed in there at the back. Putting on his gloves, he picked up the purse, then opened it. It had her wallet with her ID and all her credit cards.

He immediately took photos of it all and sent them back to Leah, with a text message saying, **No sign she was here. I think she was abducted after work.**

And, with that thought well underway, he checked behind every door and then went through the boxes. But found nothing of interest. As he headed back to the bedroom, he wondered about her cell phone. He called Leah and asked her to ring her friend's phone, so he could check if it was here.

As soon as she did, he heard noise from the bathroom, which he hadn't even checked yet. And there was her cell phone, sitting on the counter. He stared at it grimly. "If there was ever a sign that something wrong had happened, that would be it."

He didn't know anybody who would take off without their cell phone, not in this day and age. That was a lifeline to the world outside. And, in this case, she had needed it more than most. He pulled out his phone and called Leah back. "Yeah, her phone's here too," he noted grimly.

"Shit."

"I'll call you back." And, with that, he hung up and immediately went through Pamela Betts's contacts and phone numbers. He found absolutely nothing recent, and then, when he checked her texts, he saw three to the same number.

Please leave me out of this.

I don't want anything to do with this.

And a response came back. **Too late.**

And another one. **Definitely too late.**

Absolutely no quarter had been given, and he suspected that, by the time she'd handed over the information that they wanted, she'd received no relief. Particularly since she'd been trying to get out of the situation.

In this case the die had already been cast, and, whether she was willing or not, she was caught up in it.

Lachlan took multiple snapshots of the text conversations and sent it all back to the team, including Mason and Tesla. Then, with another look around, and her purse and cell phone shoved into his shirt, Lachlan headed back out again, locking the door as he left.

He made his way downstairs, without anybody seeing him, which was just another reason to be worried about these apartments with lax security. Anybody could come and go, and nobody seemed to give a damn.

What they needed was video cam feeds from here but too late for that. Besides, the hackers would have just deleted the incriminating parts of any video, just like they had already rigged the security video at work. So too late in that corner too.

As Lachlan hopped back into his vehicle, he called Leah again. "This doesn't look good."

"No, it doesn't," she murmured, her voice trembling. "Can I reroute you somewhere?"

"Sure, but where?" he asked.

"To the morgue. They picked up a Jane Doe this morning."

"Yep, I've got no problem doing that. Do you have access to any photos better than her ID?"

"Yeah, just give me a second," Leah replied.

And, with that, he punched in the coordinates to the morgue and headed off to see if he could identify a Jane Doe.

CHAPTER 6

LEAH WAITED BESIDE her phone, tense, but, when the call came through, she already knew what the answer was. "It's Pamela, isn't it?" she whispered.

"Yes, it is," Lachlan confirmed, his voice calm. "And considering the apartment and the state that I found it in, I think she was accosted outside, and either she let them in willingly or they had a key. There wasn't a single hint of damage to the door or any kind of struggle inside her apartment. Looks like she died last night sometime. The coroner is trying to pin it down closer, but we won't have that information just yet."

"No, it would be soon after she left work probably," she noted, trying to keep her voice controlled, but a sob broke free.

"I'm sorry," Lachlan added. "I gather she was your friend."

"She was somebody I worked with. Somebody I liked and a part of my team. So, yeah, she was a friend. And I'm really fed up with all this bullshit happening," she snapped, her weepy voice gaining strength. "What the hell do we have to do to get answers?"

"You tell me," he replied, with a note of gentle amusement. "This is your show now."

"It sure is," she snapped bitterly. "I need her phone."

"Yeah, I'm bringing it back," he confirmed. "I'm not exactly sure how much information you'll find on it though."

"It doesn't matter," she argued. "I'll find whatever there is, and, from there, we'll find the next step." She was silent for a moment, then asked, "Where was she found?"

"In an alley a couple blocks away from her place," he told her quietly.

"They just threw her away like garbage, *huh*?" She tried hard to keep the bitterness out of her voice, and then she didn't even bother with that. "Sometimes I really hate people." Then she hung up the phone. She quickly relayed the information to the others on her team and sat here for a long moment.

She shook her head. "Dammit, Betts, I'm sorry. I don't know what the hell you got yourself into, but obviously you were trying to get out, and, for that, I'm sad that you didn't make it."

And she was. Pamela had been a good person, no matter where she may have taken a wrong turn. Everybody was entitled to take a wrong turn sometime, and, in this case, well, it seemed like the wrong turn had been fatal. All Leah could think about was how her projection of the next bank target, and the names of people related to that bank and others of interest, had been pertinent to someone—someone willing to kill for that info.

And it's the only case that Pamela had been working on, as far as Leah knew. But, with that thought in mind, she headed into Betts's computer accounts, wishing she were at the office, where she could check on Betts's searches and her history. She phoned her boss and suggested that somebody needed to search Betts's computer to see just what she'd been up to.

"I've already got somebody on it," he replied, "but they're having trouble accessing her accounts."

"That's not good either," she stated. "Is somebody trying to hack in there?"

"That's what we're afraid of right now," he noted wearily. "Believe me. We're on it."

"You might be on it," she noted, "but I think somebody is way ahead of us. What was she working on?"

"This bank case," he told her. "The same case we're all working on. I don't know what these hackers could be after."

"The only thing they can be after is the little bit we already know," Leah suggested. "And unfortunately that isn't enough to cause anybody to do anything but laugh at us."

"Hey," her boss said, "hold the bitterness, would you?"

"Yeah, sure," she murmured. "I'm trying."

"We did do a rundown on your target bank's employees."

"Good. Is everybody accounted for?" He hesitated, and she closed her eyes. "Of course not. Someone is missing, aren't they?"

"One."

"And where is that person?"

"Nobody knows," he replied calmly. "So there is a chance that it's happening again."

"A chance? Really? You know better," she stated, "but nobody would listen to me." And, with that, she hung up, feeling completely sick and frustrated. She stared off into the corner, and, when Axel walked in, she looked over at him and shrugged. "How do you guys do this all the time?"

"We like to think that just enough successes keep us going," he explained, "but the truth is, sometimes it's hard.

Sometimes things go well, and sometimes they don't go well at all." He shrugged. "And some of these missions, cases, or events, whatever you want to call them, can be downright ugly."

She stared at him, then pulled herself together. "Would you mind putting on coffee?" she asked. "I've got some hacking to do." She wasn't sure what she was looking for, but, when she found it ten minutes later, she stared at it in shock.

Walking in with a cup of fresh coffee, Axel took one look at her face and asked, "What?"

"Looks like Pamela found names and addresses of everybody on the boards of various German banks and their contact information," she stated. "That's what her search was all about."

"Can you tell if she printed it off?"

"Wouldn't matter if she had or not," Leah noted. "Her cell phone could have taken screenshot after screenshot, and she would have immediately sent it and then deleted those. She could have emailed it, and it doesn't even matter at this point in time." Leah shook her head and sighed. "The bottom line is whether the hackers needed that information. I don't know, but she collected it."

"What else did she collect?"

"The information we used for my analysis on the first two banks that were hit. And the bank that everybody else thought would get hit," she added, with a huff, "but not the one that I thought was next."

"So everyone thought you were wrong and ignored your target bank?"

"Seems like it. I don't know." Leah stared at the information in confusion. "Or Pamela just didn't get that far in sharing the data." She turned to face him, her expression grim. "But one employee from my target bank is already missing, confirmed by my boss." She shook her head, turning around again. He waited, letting her work, as she pounded her keyboard. Finally she shrugged. "I have no idea what Pamela did with this data. I also don't know if she managed to distribute all this information."

"But like you said, even a screenshot would have done it," Axel replied.

She nodded. "In theory, yes. And that just makes me feel even shittier."

"It's got nothing to do with you," he noted.

"I personally vetted her," she murmured. "I should have realized that she was struggling when she talked about needing to leave the industry."

"And instead you probably took the other path and tried to commiserate with her and tell her it would be fine and that things would get better. Right?"

"Yeah. It sounds like you've been there."

"I think we all have," he agreed quietly. "Not everybody is cut out for this kind of a life."

"Is anybody?" she asked bitterly. "I mean, I get it, and I know that I'm doing valuable work, but, at the moment, that's feeling very thin."

"Of course it is," he noted. "One of your friends is dead, and you feel responsible."

She nodded. "And yet I know it's stupid, and I shouldn't feel responsible. I mean, whatever she did, she did on her own. Yet, at the same time, that's how I feel."

"Of course," he replied gently. "And you also know that's a perfectly normal reaction."

"Maybe," she murmured, "but is it normal to feel betrayed?"

"You are feeling both because it hasn't ever happened to you before," Axel explained calmly. "And, for that, I'm grateful for your sake because it sucks. And there's absolutely nothing you can do about it but keep up the good fight."

She shook her head. "I'm not even sure I know how to do that."

He handed her the coffee he had brought for her.

She stared at it for a long moment and then nodded. "Okay, so what do we know? We know that somebody on my team of analysts was collecting information these hacker guys wanted, and we'll assume that she also handed them all the other information we had garnered about who these black-hat hackers could be and how we thought the kidnappers were local hires and the victims of the kidnappers were decoys and what bank we thought they would hit next. How the hackers were the primary element of the main actors and their motivation was driving this operation. How the kidnappers were more of a diversion and just local hires. The top tier versus the lower rung."

He nodded. "Yeah, we have to take that as a given. So the next question is, since the hackers probably have your analysis and notes, do you want to change your analysis?"

She stared at him for a long moment. "As in, now that they know I've called out their target bank, the hackers will abort and choose another? But if they have that missing person... I'll have to think about that. And what is it that these hacker guys are after with all this? After all, they are doing their own analysis of these banks. So why do they need mine? I mean, it feels personal now to attack Betts, just to get confirmation of what they were already planning to do, right?"

"That's because it is personal now," he agreed, with a nod. "A friend of yours is dead. Yes, she took a wrong turn in life, but she's dead nonetheless. And that's something you'll have to come to grips with."

"You're not kidding," she murmured. "It's such a personal betrayal since I'm the one who gave her clearance for this position. By rights, my boss did first, then I did second. But you can bet I'll be the one to take the hit over that."

"She was compromised, so you aren't responsible."

She snorted at that. "You know that nobody will give a shit about that, right?"

He smiled. "Nobody but you."

She sighed and raised both her hands, shaking her head.

"What you need to do is take another look at the information that you pulled to see if there was a close second to the primary target bank that you chose. Look at what it would take for these guys to have chosen a different bank than the one you did."

"Finding out that I expected them to be there," she noted, "that would change their target."

"But would it?" Axel asked. "Would Betts not have told them that nobody believed you?"

"Maybe, but why take a chance, when plenty of other banks are around?"

"Targeting your chosen bank," he murmured, "means that, once again, we're looking at a personal connection."

"Why that bank? … And why Pamela?" she cried out.

"Because they could," he stated instantly. "Because she was somebody they could pressure. And having done that and having gotten all docs regarding your analysis, they locked Betts down, as nothing else quite could."

"It sucks." She glared at him.

"It does, indeed. And it doesn't change anything one bit."

She groaned. "I really liked her."

"Don't stop liking her just because you think she ended up doing something wrong. You don't know if she was coerced into it or if she was just desperate for a bit of freedom."

"I know." Leah stared down at the material on her computer. "What I don't know is if she told them about that particular bank." Then she stopped, frowned. "Wait. I'm not sure that Pamela had access to that information."

"What do you mean?"

"I'd just gotten out of the meeting with the higher-ups late at night, and they told me no, that they wouldn't run with my analysis. That it was not practical, not reasonable. And then I went home, crashed, woke up to my alarm. I came and picked up you guys the very next morning, not even going into work." She paused, frowning. "So, in theory, Pamela may not have even known that was the bank that I chose. Although it wouldn't have been hard to guess."

"It would be huge to know. Any way to find that out?"

"I can see if I can hack into her email," she murmured. "And I need to check her phone, but Lachlan has to get back first for that."

"He's on the way," Axel noted, as she went back to work.

When she lifted her head again, she heard the sound of voices. She gave her head a shake and looked up to see Lachlan walking toward her, Betts's cell phone and purse in his hands. She immediately reached out with both hands. "I'm grateful that you got these."

"I am too, but we're still missing a lot of information."

"I've checked her emails, and she did send off some information. I need to check into a few things here a little bit further."

"Like?"

"It looks to me like she was being pressured."

"That's usually the case," Lachlan agreed, "and, because the victims keep quiet, like they're supposed to per the blackmailers, they end up getting killed, and nobody could have done anything to help her in that event."

"And, even if we knew, there is no guarantee that we could have done anything in the first place either," she murmured.

"Exactly," Lachlan added, "so keep that in mind."

She gave him a determined smile. "I get it. I just feel bad that she didn't contact us so we could have *tried* something."

"Honestly," Lachlan suggested, "she was probably too terrified. Terrified of what would happen to her and her job."

"I know, but I think, in this case, chances are she'll also get other people killed," Leah noted. "She handed over contact information from every good-size bank in Germany. But that doesn't mean that she didn't hand over whatever she could get from other countries too." She turned to see who had just walked into the computer room.

Jonas nodded. "Some of that information is public knowledge but definitely not all of it, and, if she had access or could get access to more personal data, that would be a problem."

Leah winced at that. "That's one of the reasons Pamela was good at her job because she was a hacker herself."

Lachlan added, "And she may not have thought anything of it, until people started dying. That's probably what happened, and then, realizing she was ultimately responsible, she ended up wanting to run. Either they caught her before she could or they showed up with more demands. Chances are it was a combination of both." Lachlan held out a plate for her.

"What's this?" she asked suspiciously.

Lachlan snorted. "It's called a sandwich. Eat."

She stared at the massive concoction in his hands. "Only in your dreams could you call this a sandwich." She snorted. "This is a meal all in one."

"Isn't a sandwich considered a meal?" he asked her, with interest. "Besides, I like my sandwiches with some substance to them."

"If this is what you call *substance*"—she shook her head, as she stared at the mess of vegetables between two slices of bread—"I can't imagine what a big meal looks like for you."

"You've seen me eat," he noted, "and right now I want to see you eat."

She glared at him but accepted the plate. "I forgot that you're so bossy," she murmured.

"Since when have I ever been bossy to you?" he asked, with an injured note.

"Definitely right now," she stated, with a laugh. But she picked up the sandwich and looked at it with interest. "Is there anything *not* in here?"

"I couldn't fit in the kitchen sink," he teased, then picked up his own sandwich.

She laughed at his comment and watched as he took a big bite. With a shrug, she followed suit. It was so big it was hard for her to get her mouth around it, but, as soon as she started eating, she closed her eyes and nodded joyfully. "Oh, this is good."

He grinned. "See? You need food all the time. It feeds the soul."

"Yeah." She nodded. "The trouble is that it's really hard to see your way to that point, past the *food is life* part."

"Of course," he murmured. "Especially when you've only just found out what happened to a friend of yours."

She nodded. "And I can also see from the emails what happened."

"So tell me about that," he stated.

"It was all about her sister. They threatened Pamela's sister, her only living relative."

"And now there's only the sister," Lachlan noted.

At that, Leah froze and looked up at him. "Is there any way we can confirm her sister is still alive?" she asked. "It would be terrible if Betts went to all that trouble to save her, only to end up losing her anyway."

"I'm sure the coroner's office will do something about notifying next of kin," Lachlan added, "but we can always keep an eye out, in case they do find a way to contact her."

She nodded. "I don't think I should contact her myself," she murmured, "but I would like to make sure that somebody confirms that she's okay." She sat back and ate her sandwich.

"Where do you want to go from here?" he asked.

LEAH LOOKED OVER at Lachlan. "I want everybody from my target bank in protective custody," she snapped. "But it's probably already too late. They're apparently missing one person, and they're looking for him right now. We already know the hackers have him."

"And yet," Lachlan replied, "if they follow the pattern,

he's not the one in danger."

"No," she agreed, "that's true, but it will be somebody close to him."

"Ah, is that the trick?"

"I think so," she replied, "because in Pamela's emails, they're asking for connections between the banks. So, I think what we have here is, they take the one hostage, and they threaten them with the life of the other, and when they've done their job, they kill the person they deem responsible anyway."

Lachlan shook his head in disgust. "Leaving the other with the trauma of the kidnapping, the guilt of having betrayed the company in what turns out to be a failed attempt to save someone they are close to."

"Exactly," she snapped. "So, you know, they're assholes."

He smiled at her. "Remember. Nothing's fair about this."

"Maybe not," she murmured. "I just feel bad for Pamela. If she'd only told us that she was in trouble or that she'd been compromised, it could have been a different story."

"Knowing that they had already killed people in the previous target banks, you know how Pamela would have felt about her sister getting caught up in this."

"I know," Leah murmured, "and honestly I'm not sure I would have done anything differently."

"That's the problem," Lachlan noted. "As soon as it becomes about you, as soon as it becomes something that you can identify personally with, people tend to do exactly what Pamela did. They keep it to themselves, and they follow the ransom orders. They hope for the best, and you know what happens when you hope for the best when dealing with criminals? Things tend to go to shit."

Nodding, she added, "It's still so frustrating because we could have been ahead of these hackers a lot faster."

He smiled. "Now that we have her gear, you've logged in. You've checked her emails. You know how they're contacting people, and you know the hackers have all the addresses from everybody that they could possibly want. Gives us a ton more intel."

"Sure, but all that does is open us up to a ton more victims."

"So now we'll track them all down to warn them of the possible danger," he explained.

"*Great.* How many people can you muster?"

"As many as we need to," he replied. "We'll split up the list and start phoning."

She frowned. "Seriously?"

He nodded. "Yes, of course." Clearly it was not what she expected, but he didn't live in a world where one could just choose not to make phone calls because you didn't want to. "Hurry up and eat up your sandwich, then we'll get at it. We just need to know from you what it is that we're going for in terms of a script."

She shook her head. "I don't have the slightest idea." She looked horrified at the suggestion.

"We, of course, just want to confirm where they are and to warn them that they could be in danger," he added. "Yet … not cause a mass panic while we're at it," he joked.

She winced at that. "Yeah, that's the problem, isn't it? But I really don't want anybody else dead."

And that's what they did, spending the next several hours making phone calls. Some people were irritated that they actually had their personal numbers, and other people were worried enough that they planned to disappear for a few days. Lachlan got a hold of a woman who said her husband wasn't home and hadn't been home. Naturally she thought he was at work, but, when told he wasn't there, she was panicking.

Lachlan winced at that and wrote down the details. "Does anybody else happen to work at the bank with him?"

"Yes, yes," she replied, "my daughter. My daughter works there too."

"Have you had any contact with her?" he asked, raising his hand to get Leah's attention.

She immediately looked over and listened in on the conversation.

"No, she's not answering her phone either," the mother stated, and then she started to cry. "My God, is it them again?"

"Is it who again, ma'am?" he asked.

"The people who are doing this to everybody in banking," she replied. "I can't lose them. I can't lose my family! I just can't!"

"No, of course not. Let me get back to you." With that, he hung up and quickly relayed the information to the rest of the team, including Tesla. He looked over at Leah. "And, yes, they are from the target bank you were looking at."

She nodded slowly. "The missing man Ron told me about must be the father of this duo. Now we've got a missing father *and* his daughter."

"Was everybody else related?" Axel asked, coming in to join the conversation.

"Related or coworkers, but nothing as close as this," she murmured. "This has got to be painful."

"Related how?" Axel asked gently, pulling her back to the conversation.

"I think one was an ex-wife, and one was a cousin," she replied, trying to clear her head.

"Okay, so now we have a father and daughter. And what happened in the other cases?"

"You know what happened," she snapped. "The person kidnapped is not the one who was killed."

"So, in this case we don't know who was kidnapped, since both father and daughter are missing, or at least unaccounted for at the moment," Lachlan clarified. "And we need to get a hold of the bank to find out if they're actually missing and not just avoiding calls or busy getting yelled at in a staff meeting or something."

She nodded. "That's true," she murmured. With that, she phoned her boss and started to get things in motion. "The question really is," she told Lachlan and Jonas, once she was off the phone, "how do we stop them?"

"How to stop them," Lachlan stated, with a nod to Jonas, "is a completely different issue entirely. If they already have the father, then chances are things are in motion that will be almost impossible to stop."

"I agree," Jonas added.

She stared at them. "That is not acceptable."

Lachlan smiled at her. "I'm glad to hear that fire and strong tone back in your voice."

She gave her head a shake. "Okay, so I may have lost it for a little bit there, but I can't have them taking out the father or the daughter."

"So, would anybody have known that the daughter worked there?" Axel asked.

"I'm sure people did, but, in a lot of cases, they would have kept it very quiet and low-key. It's standard procedure in a bank. Your first day on the job, they tell you what to do if there is a robbery or the like. And sharing the same last name is risky in a bank. But she may be married, with a different last name. However, obviously the hackers know. The hackers also know that the father is just an employee of the bank. He's not the owner of the bank or the CEO."

"Chances are the person who's masterminding all this has a beef with this smaller bank in particular," Lachlan suggested. "And it's too early to know just what that beef could be."

"Not necessarily," Axel interjected "I'm pretty sure we can go to the other banks and find out if they've got any disgruntled employees or dissatisfied customers. Every company has them." He turned and looked at Leah. "Surely you guys did that already."

"You'll have to ask my boss," she replied. "I didn't handle any of that end of it."

Axel nodded and immediately pulled out his phone.

Just then, a series of sirens went off.

"Stay here." Lachlan bolted to his feet and disappeared, racing down the hallway to the weapons room. As soon as he got there, he pulled out handguns for himself, tucking one into his boot, then handed two more to Axel.

Jonas came racing behind them. Once he saw the weapons, he rubbed his hands together and snatched a couple for himself.

"I'm not sure you should even have any of these," Lachlan admonished him.

"Too bad," Jonas replied. "You wouldn't want to leave a friendly neighborhood guy like me defenseless, would you?"

"Didn't you tell someone you have some weapons?" Lachlan asked in a mock grin.

"Hey, none that I'm allowed to use," he admitted, "at

least not officially. But, like you, who the hell wants to travel in this world without one?"

And, on that note, Lachlan raced back to the computer room. "Head into your bedroom, and don't come out."

"What do we think it is?" she asked, as she raced toward her bedroom.

"I don't know," he murmured, "but they will not get to you."

"What about you?" she asked, looking worried.

He grinned at her. "And here I thought you didn't care."

She glared at him. "I don't want anybody else killed," she announced.

"Keep that thought uppermost," he murmured. "And hopefully we'll get through this without a fight. If we're lucky, that alarm has already scared off anybody who was planning to enter."

"I doubt it," she argued, somewhat bitterly, "considering what we've already been through."

"Exactly," he agreed, "so stay calm, stay quiet, and stay low." And, with that, he was gone.

CHAPTER 7

LEAH, BACK IN her bedroom, with her secured laptop in bed with her, quickly brought up the safe house's security cameras on the screen. Everybody thought that having security cameras kept you safe, but what they tended to forget about was the fact that anybody—like hackers— who could actually get access to the security camera could do whatever the hell they liked with them.

The good guys were heading to the front door and likely beyond. She checked the cameras in the second floor hallway, and, when she saw no sign of anyone, she moved down to the garage. She wasn't sure exactly where danger was set to trigger from, but she could find out easily enough. It would just take a few clicks, but, in the meantime, she needed to know if anyone was inside.

She heard the men talking to themselves. She didn't know if they'd picked up some kind of mic or headset system, but she wished they had included her.

And then she chuckled. She didn't need them to include her. She would include herself, invited or not. It took a little bit longer to find the frequency that they were working on, but, as soon as she got it and heard them talking, she butted in. "The security cameras are clear," she stated bluntly. "Nobody is in the upstairs hallway. I'm checking the garage and parking area now."

There was dead silence on the other side for a few seconds, and then Lachlan's voice, calm and measured, replied, "Presumably you're still in your room?"

"Yep, I sure am," she snapped. "I was off my game before, and, for that, I'm sorry. But I'm back. And believe me. I won't just be a sitting duck for some asshole to come through and punch my clock before I'm ready. Okay, the garage is clear," she confirmed. "You guys are free to go out."

"Gee, thanks." Lachlan's tone was dry.

She grinned, completely unrepentant. "You could have asked earlier."

"And we could have checked it for ourselves."

"You could have, but you didn't get there fast enough," she teased.

"Yeah, remind me about that later," Lachlan stated.

"Not likely," she replied. "You'll probably just yell at me."

"Why would I yell at you?" he asked in astonishment.

She stopped, thought about it, and asked, "You wouldn't?"

"No, and, whenever you can help, then help away," he noted. "As a matter of fact, if you can track where that trigger in the system was tripped, chances are we'll find out who is behind this."

"I doubt it," she noted, "but I've already found something. Somebody did hack the system and set off an alarm at just about that time we heard the siren, but they did it remotely."

At that, Jonas repeated, "Remotely? That's not good."

"It's both good and bad," she explained. "I mean, … it means hackers are here in Germany that we probably haven't seen before, which isn't good." She sighed, then continued.

"At the same time, it does give you a better idea of what we're dealing with now."

Lachlan said to his team, "We need to make a run through the streets and around the blocks."

"Yeah, I'm already on the street cameras," Leah replied, sounding distracted. "I'll keep you on the mic, so you can talk to me," she noted. "Stay safe, y'all." And, with that, she fell back to check once more into the safe house's security cameras. She did a full sweep on the garage for the last hour and even the first floor but couldn't see any activity.

The only thing she saw was Axel entering, coming in with breakfast, and that was several hours ago. Frowning, she kept going and then checked outside to look for security cams on the exterior of this building. Surely there would be some cameras set up outside of a safe house. It didn't take long to find those either.

That was a problem.

If it hadn't taken her long, it wouldn't take any other hacker very long, and that was something they needed to fix—and fast. She didn't want to stay somewhere that anybody could hack, and, if anybody would be hacked, it couldn't be her. She went back four hours and watched the vehicles on the street parked out in front, keeping the feedback slow. This area was a mix of commercial and residential. She watched as a vehicle pulled up, ... a black SUV with shadowed windows.

"If there was ever anything quite suspicious, it's that," she muttered, wondering why everybody always had such stereotypical vehicles. But they probably did it because it worked, and right now she would do a lot to see inside those windows.

As she watched, one man got out of the vehicle and

walked across the street. He went inside a small café and came out about ten minutes later, carrying two cups of coffee. Two cups. One for him and one for a friend or whatever. She frowned because that seemed so innocent, and so perfectly normal that she had to wonder why she was even watching it.

Except, that it was also as abnormal as you could get in this current situation. He got into the passenger side of vehicle, juggling the two cups, which further confirmed that somebody else was also in there with him. The driver obviously. Somebody who was likely on watch.

They had stayed for another hour and then slowly drove away. She took note of the license plate and backtracked so she could get a picture of his face. But nothing was clear, and nothing was definitive about any of it. She hooked on to a video camera outside the cafe to see if she could get a better picture of his face. As soon as she got one, she ran it through a database. Something was vaguely familiar about his face, but she couldn't quite place it.

As she kept that run open, her laptop complained about the increase in power usage. She swore at that. "I know. I know. I should be back in my office, with a good piece of equipment," she muttered. "But, hey, we'll get through this."

She kept working away on other cameras but found absolutely nothing to be seen. She went back to the origination of the signal that had triggered the alarm, and, outside of the fact that it had been done remotely, and, giving it as much as she could, she still couldn't trace it. The failure just pissed her off more.

Shaking her head at the mess that she found herself in, her laptop suddenly beeped. She checked out the search that she'd done and frowned. "Now that's interesting," she murmured.

"What's interesting?" Lachlan asked through her head-set, reminding her that, as they were still connected to her, she was still connected to them.

"So one of the board members from the smaller bank, the one that I tagged as being the next likely target," she explained, "was on a camera earlier, getting out of a black SUV with tinted windows, then went into a coffee shop and came back with two cups and sat inside the vehicle for an hour before pulling away."

"Did you get a license plate?"

"I did, and I nabbed a photo of the man from the street cameras," she murmured. "I just don't know why he and the driver of the SUV sat there for an hour."

"Is this board member also the CEO of that target bank, plus the father who's missing?"

"I'm running facial recognition now, hoping to verify that," she said. "And, yes, it is."

"So, he's not necessarily missing."

"Maybe not," she muttered. "At least not then. I wasn't able to see who else was inside the vehicle."

"No, and chances are you won't. It could be the hackers who were setting it in motion, or somebody blackmailing him, but it could also be some private business deal, and they didn't want anybody close enough to listen in."

"Sure," she agreed, "but just because they were there in the SUV doesn't mean that people can't listen in."

"But no way now to get a hold of any information on it, is there?"

"No, not right now." She frowned. "I'm still trying to figure out why he would have been there though. I mean, it's literally just up the street from here."

"Trying to figure that out won't be the easiest thing either," Lachlan noted, "but run a search and see if you can find out where that vehicle is now. We'd like to have a talk with him regardless."

"So, if he's the father of the father-daughter duo employed by that target bank, then we still need to find the daughter too," Axel noted.

"Yes, well—" Leah stopped and added, "I wonder if the daughter was in there in the SUV with him."

"It's possible," Axel agreed. "Have you done a full search on the family to see if they need money?"

"No, in any scenario like this, they should already have plenty of money."

"And yet somebody is ripping off these banks," he reminded her.

"I know," she replied, "and that's frustrating too."

"It definitely is, but we don't know what we're up against," Lachlan added, "so let's just keep all options open."

"I'm worried about the daughter," she stated abruptly.

"Track down that vehicle through the cameras systems and see if you can come up with a current location, so we can hit it," Lachlan replied.

"What are you guys doing now?" she asked, even as she worked her keyboard.

"Not much until you find us something," Lachlan noted cheerfully.

"I'm searching through the city cameras for the SUV," she stated simply. "I guess we're not very far away from his bank, so it's not out of the realm of possibility that he had an early morning meeting before going to work."

"Check to see if he ever showed up before then," Lachlan stated. "When did you say it was?"

"It was earlier," she replied, "somewhere around the time that Axel came in with the groceries."

"So, it could have been just in time to go to work," he muttered. "I'd still like to find the daughter."

"Yeah, me too," she stated quietly. "And it does make me suspicious that maybe he's in on it."

"Just because the man had coffee doesn't mean anything," Lachlan replied, cautioning her.

"I know. I know," she agreed, "but it doesn't make me feel much better."

"Let's just try to stay focused."

She sighed. "This isn't exactly how I planned to spend my week."

"Hey, just think of it as a small holiday."

"Right, I still don't have a change of clothes. I still don't have access to my own home and my cat, or anything else to do with my own personal life," she explained. "I'm stuck in a safe house that people are hacking into, setting off alarms, and why would anybody do that again?" she cried out.

There was a moment of silence at the other end. "To get us out," Lachlan stated immediately.

"*Great*, so now you guys got out, and you've left me alone."

"Yes," he replied.

Something in his voice got to her. "Did you know that would happen?" she cried out.

"I knew it was a possibility," he stated cautiously. "It always is."

"Well, crap," she said, "that doesn't make me feel any better."

"You have the cameras on though, and you've hacked into the system," he reminded her, "so you can see somebody coming."

"It's not that easy," she immediately countered. "I mean, if somebody has hacked into the system to set off the alarm, you can bet that they can shut it down, so they can enter."

"Seriously?" he asked. "You won't see them coming?"

"Not if they're any good," she replied. "And the fact that they've done what they've already done suggests that they are probably pretty good."

"In that case," Lachlan stated, "I'm coming back."

"Then they'll see you, and it will be a whole different story."

"So what you want me to do?"

"I don't know," she replied in frustration. "Do whatever you're doing." She hammered away at the keyboard.

"Are you sure?"

"Yes. No! I don't know. It's confusing as shit. I'm doing what I'm doing—hacking into our own system to see if anybody was here before me—and maybe nobody is coming here at all."

He hesitated, considering that. "I'm not far away," he added. "That was never my intention."

"Maybe not, but that doesn't mean it's not somebody else's."

"No, you're right there," he agreed. "I'll be back in, say, fifteen minutes."

"Fine," she muttered and heard him discussing something with the others, but it wasn't loud enough for her to pick up on it. Just then her laptop started beeping again.

"What's that?" he asked in her ear.

"I'm busy. Go away," she snapped, still frantically typing.

He chuckled. "That's what I like. When you get your

chutzpa back, you get it back in a big way."

She snorted at that. "What do you know about it?"

"You'd be surprised."

Lachlan sounded so utterly confident that she shook her head. "Tesla would never have said anything about my temper."

But there was just enough doubt in her voice that he had to laugh.

"Fine," she added, "of course she would have."

"Don't worry. I'm used to people with tempers."

"Yeah, well, how come? Do you have one?" She hadn't stopped typing.

"Not really. I'm one of those fairly laid-back types."

"And that just pisses me off even more," she stated. "Nobody likes someone who's perfect."

At that, Lachlan laughed again.

"Go away," Leah repeated. "You're distracting me."

"Oh, that's interesting. In what way do I distract you?"

"Oh no, you don't," she replied. "Go away."

And, with that, he agreed. "Okay, I'll be quiet for a while. But tell me if anything comes up." And there was a sharpness to his tone, as if he feared she would go off on her own.

"Don't worry," she replied. "I don't have a death wish."

"Good. I don't want to have to explain to Tesla that I didn't look after you."

That made her stop. "She didn't send you over to look after me, did she?" She lifted her gaze from the laptop to stare into space, while she considered that.

"No. More to just keep an eye on things," he replied, laughter in his voice.

"Ha! Knowing her, there was probably an ulterior motive."

There was silence on the other end, and, with his tone a little too neutral, he asked, "What kind of ulterior motive?"

"She's been trying to get me married off for a long time," she explained. "I just don't bite."

"Why not?" Lachlan asked. "Or maybe you bite too much?"

"Ouch," she muttered, typing harder now.

"Not trying to be mean," he replied, "but, if she's putting all these great guys in front of you, how come you don't like any of them?"

"Maybe I'm just not ready to be married or to be married off to just anybody," she snapped, then paused. "But everybody who's happily married always wants everybody else in the world to be in the exact same stage, which I find especially irritating."

He burst out laughing. "You know what? I get that a lot too," he confirmed. "I have friends who are happily married, and they keep telling me that I should do the same. I've heard it over and over again that life will never be the same if I find the right person."

"Right. Everybody who is married always has this impression that it's so easy to find the right person."

"Yeah, because they found that happiness, so they think if they can, anybody can."

"That's bullshit too," she snapped. "It's not like the right person is just tripping over my life to get to me." He chuckled, and then she stated bitterly, "You are supposed to be quiet."

"Yes, ma'am," he replied immediately.

Leah groaned. "I think … I like you," she murmured, "but sometimes you're very, very irritating."

"Yep," he agreed. "That's quite all right, and I don't imagine you're much better."

She gasped at that, but then he went silent. She wondered why and then started to worry. "You still there?" she asked cautiously.

"I am," he said, his voice low. "Stay quiet." She didn't know what the hell was going on until suddenly he whispered, "You have company."

"*Great*," she muttered, "I can't see anything on the video cameras."

"You said earlier that somebody who hacked in can possibly control them."

"Well, if they are, … they're doing a damn good job," she muttered, as she clicked away on her computer.

"The elevator is moving," he shared.

"How do you know?" she asked, bolting to her feet. "Shit, of course it's moving."

"Can you hear it?"

"No, I can't hear anything," she muttered. "But that shouldn't be happening. Somebody hacking the elevators, I should find. … Unless they are using a completely different route."

"I'm sure they are," he agreed quietly.

"It's also one of those cases of somebody else's ideas working better than mine."

"What would yours do?" he asked softly.

"I was trying to shut down the elevator, and then the only person who could get up here would need permission." She kept clicking away, feeling the pressure build. "I think I shut down the elevator now." As she watched her computer screen, another series of clicks came. "Shit, they just brought it up again."

"So somebody is online and hacking it right now?" he asked in a sharp tone.

"Yes," she said. "I'll need a hand here."

"Yeah, I'm already here," he confirmed. "Stay put."

"Yeah, I'm staying put all right," she muttered. "But I'll find this asshole. I really don't like when somebody tries to take over control of my computer."

And, with a laughing tone in his voice, Lachlan noted, "Understood."

"Yeah, you can laugh," she replied, "but I really don't like the position I'm in."

"And, like I said, I'm right here," he said.

As she looked up, there he was. She frowned at him. "What the hell? Where did you … How the bloody hell did you get back inside without me seeing you?"

"I stayed out of camera range at the second-floor landing," he explained. "I was up and down the hallway where you couldn't see me because I knew we had somebody coming in."

It took her a moment to even begin to process that. She shook her head at the audacity of whoever was out there. "Okay, that won't happen again," she declared, as she worked away on the keyboard.

"But now we don't have any eyes or ears on the outside."

"What about the other two?"

"They've gone hunting."

"Good, as long as nobody knows they're out hunting, maybe they'll actually get somewhere."

"But that means you have to trust me to handle whatever is coming through that door."

"I trust *you*," she stated, "and I also know that there's no guarantee that whatever's coming through the door is actually something you can handle." She looked up at him. "So be careful."

He nodded. "Always."

And, with that, she had to be satisfied, as he slipped back down the hallway. Just then an explosion sounded.

Everything on her laptop went blank.

LACHLAN HAD JUST barely ducked into a first-floor closet when the front door blew. Immediately two men stormed in, guns drawn. They were dressed in black, hoods over their heads. They raced into the living room, but as the one man went around the front of the living room, Lachlan nabbed the second one and knocked him out. Then he came around the corner to see Leah standing there in the first floor hallway, her hands up, facing the gunman.

She cried out, "What do you want? What is this madness?" she asked. "Who are you?"

"You're the analyst." She stared at him eerily, and he gave her a rough shake. "Are you the analyst?"

And then she nodded. "I'm an analyst," she confirmed. "Why?"

"Because you're wanted somewhere," he replied, and she was grabbed and pulled roughly forward.

She struggled. "I don't want to go anywhere with you."

"That's just too damn bad," he said, with a sneer. "You stuck your nose into something that wasn't your business. Now people want to talk to you."

That wasn't anything she was interested in doing right now, not this way.

Stepping behind the guy, Lachlan's handgun jammed against the small of the intruder's back. Lachlan spoke to the gunman. "I'd listen to the lady if I were you. She doesn't want to go anywhere just now."

The gunman froze. "Shit. Where's Tori?"

"If you mean the guy who came in with you, he's having a nice nap in the front closet."

"Shit. What a fuckup."

"Yep, it sure is," Lachlan muttered. "Now drop the weapon."

"Hell no. You're not taking me in."

"Why not?" Lachlan asked.

"Because people die in custody."

"Are you kidding me? You guys are killing people left, right, and center."

The man gave a surprise start, but he never said anything, and Lachlan had to wonder at that. Maybe they had gotten something wrong here, but first he looked over at Leah. "Are you okay?"

She nodded mutely. "I still don't understand why they would want me," she cried out. "He said that I had stuck my nose into something, but I don't really know what's going on."

Lachlan replied calmly, "That's not the issue right now. Let's just get this guy secured."

And, with that, rather than arguing with Lachlan, in a swift move, she lifted the handgun that the gunman still held, while Lachlan butted him hard in the head, taking him to his knees. With him on his knees, Lachlan dropped him all the way to the floor with his next blow. He asked Leah, "Will you go into the kitchen and find something to tie him up with?"

She looked at the unconscious man on the floor and nodded, then promptly left.

Grim, and in foul mood, Lachlan quickly sent a text to Axel and Jonas and Tesla, letting them know he was back, and he had two men apprehended, who had stormed the safe house to abduct Leah. He looked up as Leah raced back from the kitchen with zap straps.

He grinned. "Gotta love these things." He laced two together, so it was long enough to go around the man's wrists when tied together. Then, doing the same with two more, he tied up the man's ankles. He snatched four more out of the package, then raced to the hallway closet.

She came up behind him and, as he bent down over the man's back, she noted, "God, what if he had woken up already?"

"I've seen some guys go down and almost jump back up," Lachlan admitted. "No way to know. But this one? He looks to be down for the count."

"Thankfully," she noted, as she jerked the man's head up to get a look. She frowned. "I don't recognize him at all."

"That's a good thing," Lachlan replied.

"Maybe," she muttered, "but it would at least let me know if it was somebody in Pamela's world."

"But would it?" Lachlan asked, turning to face her. "Your good friend Pamela Betts had something going on. So let me ask you this. … Were you actually that close?"

"I knew about her boyfriend," she replied cautiously.

With both men secured, Lachlan dragged the one to drop beside the other. Then he rolled them over, so he could take pictures of their faces and sent them on to Mason and Tesla.

She stared at the men and shook her head. "No, you're right. I probably wouldn't know anybody in her world." She stared at him, her bottom lip quivering.

He looked at her in alarm. "You won't cry, will you?"

Almost immediately she firmed up and glared at him. "Of course not, but somebody I know did just die. I haven't had time to even process that."

"I get that," he replied, "and I'm sorry, but it doesn't change the fact that she was also compromised."

Leah shut down at that.

"Did we ever find her sister?" he asked her.

Leah pulled out her phone and sent off a text. When it buzzed a moment later, she nodded. "The sister is in boarding school and is confirmed to still be in attendance."

"Good, so that one has been nullified."

"Maybe," she muttered. "But how safe is she?"

"There's nobody else to pay, nobody else to pressure on her behalf, so, in all likelihood, she's quite fine now," he suggested.

"These two were looking for *the analyst. Sticking my nose in something that I wasn't supposed to.*"

He nodded. "Which makes sense."

"Says you." She snorted. "All I'm doing is my job."

"Same difference to them," Lachlan noted. "It doesn't matter to these hackers or especially these kidnappers-for-hire if it's your job or not. As far as they're concerned, you're getting in their way."

"Maybe, but I never did anything to the hackers or their hired guns," she muttered.

He laughed. "Obviously you are impacting them in some way. ... Otherwise they wouldn't be pissed off."

"I guess that's a good thing then, isn't it?" she said brightly.

"It is, indeed, and it's a good thing that we have some progress now. I'd still like to find that father and daughter."

"Me too," she muttered. "I was supposed to do that search when the alarms went off. I'll do that. See if I can find that same SUV. Particularly if they are still sitting outside on this block."

"But, like you said, we're not far away from where the father and the daughter work."

At that, her phone buzzed with an incoming text. "Tesla confirms that the father never did show up at work today."

"Interesting," Lachlan murmured. "You're sure it was him going into the coffee shop?"

She nodded. "Facial recognition software identified him, then I verified it. So I don't understand what that means."

"It's quite possible that the missing daughter was in the vehicle with him. Maybe he was sent in to get coffee as a test to see if he would be a good boy or not, and they kept the daughter in the car."

"But, in the other bank attacks," she argued, "they didn't kidnap the person they were using as leverage against the kidnapped victim."

"So something has changed in this one," Lachlan stated, "and I have a good idea why."

She stared at him, not comprehending. "What? What changed?"

He flashed her a tight grin. "You."

CHAPTER 8

LEAH SHOOK HER head. "I didn't do anything yet."

"You've obviously disrupted their pattern, now that they know we're on to them."

"And yet why go ahead with it?" she asked.

"They must have a really good reason for doing all this, what with the increased chances that they'll be caught," he noted quietly.

"And, if they managed to pull it off, I wouldn't be at all surprised if it's their last job, if they get a decent amount of money out of it and just disappear," she announced, staring at him.

"If it is good money that they don't intend to let go of, then they won't want to share it."

"So, no honor among thieves?"

"None that I've ever seen," he said, with a nod. Just then his phone buzzed. He looked down to see a text message from Tesla. "Axel and Jonas are on their way back."

"Good, so at least they're safe."

"They are, and they have some news."

"Good," she replied. "I'm getting tired of being boxed in here. And obviously we're no longer safe here."

He gave Leah a measured glance. "Yeah, that whole *safe house* name? it's kind of a misnomer sometimes."

"You think?" she stated in a scoffing tone.

"No, seriously, they are good to a point, but eventually anyone with any skills can track us down, and we need to move."

"Since it's no longer safe—not to mention the damage at the front door from that little explosion—and we'll leave anyway, I have a suggestion," she stated. "I suggest my place. I need clothes anyway, and I want to shower and have access to my own computer equipment."

"We'll see, as soon as the guys get back," Lachlan noted.

"It really shouldn't have anything to do with them," she said in a frustrated tone.

"It doesn't," he agreed, "but we have to make a plan to get out of here quietly."

"How about we just walk out the front door, like everybody else?" she asked, glaring at him.

He turned on his charm. "I do like it when you get feisty."

She threw up her hands. "Not that again."

"Why not?"

"You're just trying to distract me."

"Yeah, well, is it working?" he asked curiously.

She didn't know what to say to that at first, so she stared at him. "Seriously?"

"Think about it," he said. "I'm not leaving until the rest of the team gets back, so there's no need to rush. We need to have a plan, and we want to ensure we only step outside to put this whole scenario to rest. We don't want to keep changing locations."

"Why not?" she asked, glaring at him. "It's got to be better than sitting here all cooped up."

"Has it been that tough?" he asked.

"Yes, and no. Fine then." She threw herself down on the

couch.

"Why don't you take a look at the cameras outside your apartment and see if it's safe."

"Oh, I can do that." She jumped up.

He smiled at that. Just like anybody else, she needed to have something to do. She needed something to channel that energy into, and she definitely had a lot of energy. She might not be all that accustomed to the type of work that he did, but she was game, and she'd certainly come up with some valuable insights, particularly about the safe house.

"And reset all the cameras, please," he called out to her upstairs.

"Already done," she yelled back.

And Lachlan knew that Leah fully understood that they couldn't really stay here any longer. It wasn't just a case of the location being compromised. The systems had also been hacked, so this no longer worked. They needed to find a place to go to that would put them back under the radar again. She also needed clothes.

When the alert sounded at the back door, Lachlan quickly bypassed it and checked the camera that she had reset and let Axel and Jonas back in.

Leah soon joined them as Axel and Jonas came in with bags of groceries. She stared at them, nonplussed.

Axel flashed her a bright smile. "Hey, even in times of hunts and stress, we still need to eat."

"I get that," she admitted, "but here I figured I'd be relegated to power bars or something, since we have to move now."

"Nope, not going to happen," Axel stated, "I like my groceries too much."

She just nodded and watched as he unpacked at the dining room table. "Not even a comment about the two men on the floor?"

"Kind of used to seeing shit like that," Axel said cheerfully. "Did you check your apartment?"

"Yes," she replied. "I've been running through the last couple days to see if anybody I don't recognize is coming to my place or has been there."

"No activity?"

"No," she murmured, "it looks quite safe. So I suggest we move there."

"I'm not sure about that move. We may stop by there," Axel replied, "so you can pack a bag, but, no, we're not staying there."

"Why not?" she wailed, and then glared at him. "You've been talking to Lachlan, haven't you?"

Axel laughed at that. "We always talk."

As she watched the groceries come out of the bag, she noted that it was ready-made food. She quickly went through the rest of her video on her laptop and then hopped up and walked over curiously. "What are we having?"

"This is from the Indian house around the corner."

"Sounds good," she replied.

"You didn't mention if there was anything you didn't particularly like."

"I don't remember being asked," she quipped. "Besides, I like food. I just thought you were bringing groceries."

"Not when we're on the move," he explained. "But, at the next stop, we'll have to get more in. Four of us require actual food."

"Fine," she stated, looking around, smiling at Jonas, who was already seated at the dining room table and helping himself to the food. "Where's Markus?"

"He's gone into headquarters," Axel replied.

"But I thought he'd be guarding our nonexistent front door."

Lachlan laughed. "We all are doing that now, just from inside, while eating." He smiled that smile that made her melt.

"But what's Markus doing at headquarters?" she finally thought to ask.

"He's talking to your boss right now," Axel informed her. She stared at him, and he shrugged. "Markus wanted to have a talk with Ron about your dead colleague."

"*Great*, so people are investigating behind my back," she said, looking irritated.

"No, but Markus wasn't sure that your boss was paying too much attention to any of this."

She winced at that. "The trouble is, … he handles a lot of teams, and we're short-staffed at work."

"We think it needs to be taken seriously, and, at the moment, we're not sure that Ron is doing that."

"He's very busy."

Jonas just shook his head, while he kept on eating.

"Ron needs to refocus," Axel stated quietly but with a hint of steel in his voice, "because people are dying on this case. Unless he has ten more people who are just as at risk in another case, he needs to get his priorities right. We can count on Markus to make that clear to your superior."

She gazed at him in fascination. "Markus didn't seem all that scary."

He motioned at the table. "Come and eat."

"And then what?" she asked cautiously, as she sat down.

"With any luck we'll slip over to your place and see if we can get you some clothes, and then we'll move to a new place."

She felt her stomach sink at that. "I was hoping some of this would be over soon."

"And I suspect it will be," he admitted, "but we're not quite there yet."

She nodded. "No, we aren't." She knew it was silly and immature, but it felt like everything she had hoped for wouldn't happen.

Axel said, "Don't look so sad. We'll be out of your hair soon enough."

"How can I not be sad about this whole situation?"

At that, Lachlan walked in, took one look at the food, and smiled. "Perfect." He looked over at her. "You ready to have a change of venue?"

"You know I am," she stated, "but I really wanted to go home."

"We'll stop there," he replied gently, "but we can't stay there. Not until this is over. Leah, you have to understand that they know who you are, and, if they knew you were at this safe house, then you can bet that they know all about your place and are waiting for you there."

She stared at him. "There was no one on the cameras. It wasn't showing anybody there," she replied cautiously.

He just stared at her for a long knowing moment. Then he and Jonas shared a nod and a look.

Leah winced. "Right. And, of course, I saw nothing suspicious because they could just hack in and adjust the camera feeds to show whatever they wanted." She sighed. "So then how is it that we can even go home for clothes?"

"We'll have a physical look-see first."

"So it would be better if we don't?" she asked.

"But you need clothes, I get it."

At that, she offered, "I can go into any department store and pick up a few things."

"And, if you can do that," Lachlan noted, "it would be for the best."

She nodded slowly, letting her dream of going home fade away, along with the thought that this nightmare might be close to over. At the moment, she was just thankful to be alive. "Fine. I don't have to get anything fancy. I just need a few things to get me through a couple days."

"Better make it for more than a couple days," Axel cautioned.

"Nope." She looked at Lachlan. "You just have to fix this fast." He stared at her, and she shrugged. "I can give you a few days, but I can't put my whole life on hold."

"Can't or won't?" Lachlan asked, with a wry look.

She glared at him, and Axel held up his hand. "Children, children." He was grinning too much for her to ignore it.

She sagged into her chair, taking a plate of food from Lachlan. "Fine, but it wouldn't be my first choice."

"It wouldn't be anyone's choice," Lachlan declared. "That doesn't change the fact that, right now, for obvious reasons, we can't take you home. If they could do that here"—he pointed to the blown-down front door, now prone on the hallway floor—"then you're surely not safe at your place."

"And yet you let me believe I could go home," she argued, studying him.

"Eventually, yes. Now? Hell no. I was waiting for you to come to the same conclusion we had, on your own. It's just too dangerous."

Jonas nodded, still eating without interruption.

She didn't say anything to that, since any response

would be ridiculous. Clearly it had taken her a little too long to come to that conclusion, likely because she had been holding on to the idea of home because it would mean that this was over. "So what's to become of these two?" She looked over at the two men still tied up and *napping*, courtesy of Lachlan. "Can't we make them talk somehow and get to the bottom of this?"

"They'll be transported and interviewed," Axel stated, "though it's unlikely they'll give us anything helpful."

Clearly this wouldn't be over just because she wanted it that way. "I sure hope we get to the end of this soon." She rubbed her temples with a huge sigh.

"You and everybody else," Lachlan added.

At that, she swallowed her protest because a lot of other people were involved. And, for all she knew, even someone's daughter was already in panic mode, knowing there was a chance she and her father wouldn't survive. "It's really sad," Leah murmured.

"It is. It's really sad," Lachlan agreed, "but it's not the end of the world yet."

"It is for all the victims," she argued, looking up at him, holding her fork in her hand but not eating yet. "We're just too late all the time."

"Maybe for now but that doesn't mean that it'll stay that way. We will find these guys."

She nodded, but she wasn't convinced. "They've been one step ahead of us the whole way."

"And I have to wonder how and why that is."

"I'm afraid to think so, but I've wondered if it wasn't Pamela's doing."

"That's an easy answer," Lachlan noted, "and it could be the correct one. We usually find that it's these easy answers which make the most sense. I mean, hackers can probably get at anything they want online, given enough time. But who could help these hackers get the kind of information they needed only faster? Somebody on the inside is always a good bet."

She nodded. "It still sucks though."

"It absolutely does," he murmured, "but that's not the end of the day for us."

At that, her phone rang and she stared down at it. "It's my boss."

"You may want to take that," he stated in a smooth tone.

She glared at him but answered anyway, even though she'd just taken a bite of the food. "Ron, hey. Sorry, I'm just getting a bite to eat."

"No, no, I understand. I have cleared my schedule, and we'll make this a priority."

"You mean it wasn't?" she asked in a wry tone.

"You know how crazy it's been," he replied. "And I hate to say it, but you also know, with so many things happening, I haven't been giving this my full attention."

She shook her head. Score one for Markus; he must be more intimidating than he appeared. "Understood. Hopefully at this point in time, you'll be doing everything you can."

"We're on it," he stated. "We've gone through all of Pamela's files, and unfortunately it does look like she was compromised."

"Yeah, they used her sister against her," Leah confirmed.

"Oh, you found that out already," Ron replied in surprise.

"Yes, I haven't had a whole lot to do but sit here and work, being confined and all."

Ron paused. "Do you want somebody to go to your

place and get some clothes or anything?"

She contemplated that for a long moment. "These latest gunmen hacked the elevators and camera systems here, so we can't count on the security systems in place at my apartment, as it's quite likely they've already hacked into my building's security too. If they can do things like that, ... chances are they're watching my place, so it's just not worth the risk." She sighed. "I'll just pop into a store and pick up a few things, enough to get me through this. It is actually surprising how much one can do without in a case like this."

"If you're sure?" At her agreement, he added, "Right, so what else do you need?"

"I traced an SUV on our block near the safe house at the local coffee shop. Confirmed our missing father was in this area this morning around seven-thirty a.m. Confirmed he's also the CEO of my target bank. Get someone to trace the whereabouts of that SUV now. And his daughter is missing as well, who works at the target bank. See if someone can match her face on street cams with facial recognition software. Also we need to look into everybody Pamela had contact with. I want info on every database she accessed in the last week. I know that she handed over to the bad guys all the addresses and personal contact information for every one of the larger banks in or near town, possibly for all of Germany," she noted, "but I don't know about any national or international scope."

"Okay, I can get people on all that," Ron agreed, all business now. "What else?"

"I have two men unconscious on the floor here beside me," she said. "I'll send you some photos. I need to know who they are and what connection they have to this mess. They also were after me," she noted quietly. "They called me 'the analyst,' and one of them told me that I was, quote, 'poking my nose into something that wasn't my business,' and that 'somebody wanted to talk to me,' which seems fairly specific."

"Somebody wanted to talk to you?" Ron asked.

"Yeah. I'm thinking either they want to know how far along we are on this case or else they're after some information we hadn't even looked at so far."

"Surely they would understand that we will be on their tails the whole way," Ron added.

"That is unclear for now," she replied.

"Okay. God, what a mess. I had no idea."

"Get back to me when you have something," she told Ron, before abruptly ending the call.

As soon as they had all eaten, she got up and asked the guys, "Are we ready to go?"

"Give us a second to clean up," Lachlan replied quietly, "and, yeah, we'll be ready."

She nodded, then quickly helped him clear the remains of the food. When her boss called back right away, she looked down at her phone and answered it. "Now what?" she asked, and then winced at her tone.

"Nothing so far," he replied quietly. "I was thinking about what you said, about all that you asked for help on, and I'm calling to apologize. I really owe you for this one, for taking so much onto your shoulders, and I'm sorry for not paying more attention. You take care and don't do anything stupid."

"I'm not planning on it," she said, "but you're right. This has been a pretty scary experience."

"And that's why I'm worried," he explained. "You're the best analyst we've got, plus I consider you a friend."

"Well then, could you maybe put a little more effort into keeping me alive?" she stated, trying to keep a caustic tone out of her voice.

"I will," he stated. "I'm on it."

And, with that, he hung up, and she looked over at the team with a quizzical expression. "So I gather that, despite the quiet demeanor he displayed in my presence, Markus is actually one scary dude."

Chuckles broke out all around. "Markus is a very scary dude, particularly if he sees an injustice," Axel noted, with a hint of amusement.

"He's the best," Lachlan stated, still laughing out loud.

"Ah, well, that was Ron, apologizing and telling me to stay safe."

"Any reason to believe he doesn't mean it?" Lachlan asked.

She stared at him and then winced. "You know what? I don't know the answer to that." Looking at his face, she knew that she had read his expression correctly. "Now I presume you're asking me if he could be compromised or not."

"We have to look at everybody," Lachlan repeated.

"I would hope not," she replied calmly, "but can I say that for sure? No, of course not."

"I'm glad you're not discounting it," Lachlan added quietly, "because that becomes a problem."

"No, I'm not, and I know that, in some cases, that can get pretty ugly."

"In a lot of cases it gets very ugly," he noted. "We just don't want this to be one of them."

There wasn't a whole lot she could say to that. By the time they had everything cleaned up and ready, he held out a hand. She looked at it and then cautiously reached for it.

"I love the way you're so cautious," he said, with a grin.

"Yeah, well, it feels like you're asking more of me than just to hold your hand," she admitted quietly.

He frowned. "No, I'm not. We have a team coming to pick up the men and our drivers have been switched out. We are doing everything we can to keep you safe."

She smiled. "That may be what it seems like from your side, but from here? I'm not so sure."

He grinned at her. "Let's go." He led her and the others out of the safe house and down to the garage. As soon as they were inside their new vehicle, she relaxed ever-so-slightly. "Does this one have bulletproof glass?" she asked quietly.

Jonas nodded and replied, "It does, indeed, so we should be safe."

"It's that 'should be' that bothers me," she muttered.

"Me too," he agreed cheerfully. "Yet we must deal with what we can deal with."

"Sure, but that doesn't mean it'll be good news in any way."

"You keep track of any bad news," he suggested, "and we'll keep things moving forward."

For now, she had to be satisfied with that.

AS SOON AS they pulled up to the mall, Lachlan looked over at Leah and asked, "Which store?"

She pointed to a general store off to the side, and his eyebrows popped up. "Are you sure you'll find what you need there?"

"We can access another store through there by going out the back," she explained, "and this is just the easiest way to get there."

"Good enough," he said, as he hopped out, leaving the others to wait in the vehicle.

She looked at him and asked, "Are you coming too?"

"I'm coming," he stated in a tone that allowed for absolutely no argument. She had to admit that she wasn't upset or offended about the idea but didn't know that he would enjoy the shopping much. "You know that I'm just going in to get some clothes, right?"

"And you know that one way or another we'll keep an eye on you because somebody is after you, right?"

She glared at him. "Trust you to bring back the reality of the situation." When he looked at her in surprise, she shrugged. "It would be nice to just forget about the chaos for a little bit."

"Not happening," he snapped in a hard tone. "Not if we plan on keeping you alive."

At that, there was nothing she could say. She silently marched into the general store and picked up some face wash and a hairbrush. She paid for that there, then headed out the back door, right into the next store, making a beeline for the women's section and, within minutes, had picked out several pairs of leggings, then grabbed a couple T-shirts in her size. Nothing was of good quality, and she knew that these wouldn't hold up very long, but that was fine with her. She just needed something to get through this mess.

She also picked up some underwear and socks. Then she headed over to find a sweater.

Lachlan didn't say a word, as he walked by her side. When she was done, he asked, "Is that enough?"

"I think so. I mean, I don't know how much crazier life will get, but this is what I was thinking of."

"It works for me." Lachlan quickly led her to the cashier.

"Do you think it's safe enough right now?" she asked, looking around.

"Just act natural," he murmured. "We're safe for the moment."

"Yeah, and there again is that 'for the moment' thing that really gets me."

"Of course," he agreed. "And, if we're being watched, we're being watched. Don't worry about it. Let them see us. If they see you buying clothes, maybe they'll assume that you're not going home, and they'll ease up on your apartment building."

"Is that a good thing?" she asked.

"It's probably a good thing for the other people in the building."

At that, she winced. "Jesus, I didn't even think about how this impacts them."

"It'd be good if we didn't impact them at all, but you never know," he murmured. "I'm not trying to shock or to upset you. I'm just stating the facts of life."

"I'm getting quite an education on the facts of life," she noted. "Is this what Tesla's life is like?"

"Nope, not now. She went through hell when she met up with Mason in the first place," he shared. "But there's been a fair bit of calmness in her world since."

"I'm glad to hear that," she muttered. "But then she's made a hell of a name for herself."

"She has, indeed. She's a huge asset, and they know it."

Leah nodded at that. "I'm so glad for her. I'm not so sure about my own reputation."

"Anytime you want to come back to US soil—"

"I just don't know," she interrupted, "although Tesla has

mentioned a time or two of a position close to her after my six months here are up." Leah shrugged, then added, "I also got a call from a woman named Ice a while back. Apparently she heard that I was potentially looking at a change of venue."

At that, he turned and looked at her.

"What's that look for?" she asked, stunned at his response.

"Ice is in the middle of all this stuff. She and her husband, Levi, head up a security company, and they hire a lot of good people who do the same type of work that we do. They were all in the navy at one time, and Ice is one hell of a helicopter pilot," he shared, admiration in his tone.

"So I couldn't go wrong working for them either, *huh?*"

"They do a lot of this type of thing though," he warned her, "a lot of very personal cases. They hire out their services the world over to help people who are in trouble."

"Right, so unless I want to do this kind of work and face this kind of constant stress, it wouldn't necessarily be a good idea."

"Not necessarily good or bad," he admitted. "They would look after you, and it's not like you'd be in the field much, if at all."

"That's got to be something," she noted. "I can't say I'm feeling very charitable toward my boss right now."

"No, and maybe he just needed to have a reminder."

"I owe Markus for that."

"He is really good at seeing that kind of stuff," Lachlan said. "You know? The bigger picture. It never even occurred to me that I needed to do that."

"That's because your focus is on me in the here and now," she murmured. "Whereas Markus's focus was a little bit further down the road."

"And I get that," Lachlan agreed, "but I'm kicking my-self a little for not having raged into Ron's office and dealt with it."

"Would you have done that if I'd thought about it?"

"Yes," he stated, with a definitive nod. "Sometimes these people can get way too egotistic and think that the world is their oyster. Instead of looking after the people they should be looking after, they focus on the stupid power plays; and that is just not right."

Leah shook her head. "This whole thing has me quite confused. It seems like my boss isn't doing his job. Yet I can't really blame him because I do know how insanely busy it is."

"And maybe that's how this friend of yours ended up not having anybody to talk to when she got into trouble."

"Quite possibly, which makes me feel even guiltier," she muttered.

"Why would you feel guilty?"

"Why wouldn't I?" she asked. "If I had been there for her to talk to, we might not be in this boat."

"You might not, but it could be an even worse one. It could be that they could have used you as a way to pressure her."

"Maybe, but I still feel like she'd be alive if I had been there for her."

"That will likely be something you carry to some degree for the rest of your life," he admitted, "so don't make it worse with all the *what if* possibilities. Especially not right now. Maybe you could have done something or maybe not. Either way, it's in the past. You have to move on. Maybe some good comes from it, and, in the future, maybe you can help someone you might have missed otherwise."

She was subdued, considering that, and she nodded. "It's all about learning, isn't it?"

"It is, and it's not just about learning today. It's about learning for tomorrow. It's about learning for the next occasion, and, whether you want another occasion or not," he added, "chances are, if you stay in this work, no matter who you end up working for, a similar issue may arise. The potential will always be there."

As they stepped out of the mall, he led her to the car. She appreciated the fact that his gaze didn't stop searching everywhere around them. But it also made her very aware of the fact that she had no free pass here. They would do as much as they could do, and, beyond that, there would be trouble.

She sighed, as they neared the vehicle. "I was really hoping it would be safer."

"And maybe it is," he replied, "but I won't take a chance and have something go wrong when you're as necessary to this whole thing as possible."

"I still don't get that," she murmured, as they got in the vehicle again, both of them in one of the back seats. "There were many times I would have thought that the kidnappers could have picked me up, if they'd wanted to."

"And when would that have been?" Jonas asked.

"How about when I came to collect you guys at the airport?" she asked.

"What do you think that attempt was, with the guys following us from the airport and then shooting at us?" Axel asked, looking at her in the rearview mirror, as he pulled out of the parking lot.

She stared at him. "You think that was them trying to

get a hold of me?"

"It would only make sense. Think about it. They didn't really know who we were or why we were there. Ultimately they didn't give a crap about us."

"That's not true. I mean, obviously Jonas is somebody important."

"At least he thinks so," Axel quipped, with a smile.

"Cut it, mate." Jonas snapped but with a thread of amusement in his voice.

"He is right though," Lachlan added. "As for the rest of us, we're just workers who operate all over. So odds are they wouldn't have known us from Adam from the start."

"No," she argued, "you guys are heroes."

He looked at her in surprise and then smiled. "I'll take that. Thank you."

"I mean it. Really I do. You all know what I do. I work from a desk," she stated. "I'm not on the front lines, and I'm not somebody who is very brave. You guys have shown me a completely new world. At the moment, I may not necessarily be appreciating this new world that much," she admitted, with half a smile, "but I do understand the necessity to having you guys out there."

"Good," Lachlan noted, "then you're ahead of lots of people in the world."

She nodded. "It sucks, doesn't it?"

"It really does sometimes," he replied, "because so much of the world doesn't have a clue what's going on out there. Although we do need it to stay hidden that way sometimes. Otherwise it can get way too crazy."

"And not just crazy," she muttered, "but, once you end up with people who don't understand what's really going on, they make decisions based on their own needs and not on the needs of the group."

"Exactly," he agreed, with a happy sigh. "You learn fast."

"Well, I've lost a friend.

"We've all lost somebody," Jonas noted at her side.

She turned and looked at him. He had to be in his late thirties or maybe early forties, not very old for the position he seemed to hold, but he appeared to be of an age of wisdom and experience that she wondered about. "Looks like you've seen more than your fair share of trials and issues too," she noted quietly.

He gave her a ghost of a smile. "Absolutely, as has everyone in this vehicle. Sometimes there just are no good answers to any of it. Shit happens, and you do the best you can, but sometimes that shit just keeps on happening, and you have absolutely no recourse or way to change it."

"I really don't want my life to become like that," she replied quietly.

"Good, and, with any luck, it won't," Jonas noted, "but we can't live in the world of make-believe. We have to live in the world that we have right now. That world that we have right now shows us that bad guys are everywhere, every day of the week. Out there are a whole lot of wolves in sheep's clothing," he noted. "I hate to say it, but it really sucks sometimes."

CHAPTER 9

IRED, BUT RESIGNED to the fact that she wasn't going home anytime soon, Leah sat up a little bit. "We've been driving for a long time," she murmured. "Is everything okay?"

"Everything is fine," Axel replied.

"Not sure I believe you," she muttered.

He laughed. "Why would you say that to me?" he asked, with a big smile. "Have I ever steered you wrong?"

"I don't exactly know yet," she said. "The jury is out on that one."

Everybody grinned because any chance for humor in a situation like this was a godsend. Acceptance of what was going on would make them all feel a bit better. Looking around, she stated, "I feel like we're wasting time, and I need to get back to my laptop."

"If we're wasting time, we'll find out pretty darn fast," Axel explained, "but I would hope not."

She frowned, as if not really getting what he meant by that. "Are we being followed again?" she asked cautiously.

"We are," he replied.

"Ah, so that's what we're doing. We're going the long way, trying to lose them."

"I think I lost them a while ago," Axel noted, "but I'm not driving to our new location until I'm actually sure."

She looked over at Lachlan, and he smiled at her. "It's all good ... really."

"It's a good thing I trust you."

"It is, indeed." He smiled.

"I'm not all that good about trusting, you know?" she told him.

"Why not?" he asked, both out of curiosity and likely to keep her mind off what was happening around them.

"Things have gone wrong too many times. I mean, just look at the case with my boss."

"I'm not terribly impressed with him anyway."

"I think he's just overworked, like the rest of us," she replied.

"And I think you give him too much credit. And he's not doing you any favors. However, if you are interested in changing jobs, it doesn't sound like you're short on opportunities."

"No, probably not." She frowned, "I just ... I don't know that I'm ready to make that kind of a decision. I'm still new here."

"We came over, thinking we were doing computer training for Tesla," Lachlan explained. "So this hasn't exactly been the kind of job we thought we were heading for either."

"Yeah, I'm hoping you'll stay afterward, and we can get to that," she replied. "But, if not, you'll have to come back."

"I don't mind coming back," Lachlan noted instantly.

She grinned at him. "That was a little too easy."

"Nope, not a *little* too easy." He laughed. "It was a lot easy. It's not hard to make those kinds of decisions."

She looked at him. "I don't tend to make fast decisions."

"I don't know," he pointed out. "You do appear to trust people quickly, even if, as you say, you have a problem with trust."

"Maybe I shouldn't"—she glared at him—"but you guys are not the easiest people to work with."

At that, Axel chipped in. "Hey, I thought we'd been pretty good to work with," he argued.

"How can you even say that to me?" She sighed. "You've been easy, but your friend here? … He's a different story."

"Oh, so that's it," Axel replied, clearly enjoying the moment. "What's Lachlan done to upset you? The man usually has a silver tongue."

"Maybe too silver," she stated, with a nod. "It's way too easy to like him."

"And that's a problem? How?" Lachlan asked in amazement.

"Absolutely. Silver tongues are definitely not trustworthy."

"Whoa, whoa, whoa," Lachlan said. "How come, all of a sudden, I feel like I'm being stereotyped?"

She turned and stared at him. "If you feel that way, perhaps you are. Maybe there's also a good reason for that."

When the vehicle made a series of sharp turns again, she winced. "Oh, here we go again. I remember this maneuver all too well," she murmured.

Lachlan nodded slowly. "Maybe, but we're doing what we need to do."

"Oh, I get it," she noted. "It's just frustrating."

All of a sudden, gunfire erupted around them. She shrieked and was thrown to the floor, her head covered. She shuddered. "What the hell is that?" she whispered.

Lachlan held her head down. "Just stay down."

She peered up to see him, staring all around, but his head wasn't down. She glared at him. "If your head is not down, why should mine be?" she snapped.

"Because, if you want to live, you'll do everything I say, without argument, without hesitation, especially when gunfire is involved," he stated in a hard tone.

Of course she would. This wasn't her forte, and she didn't have a clue how to handle this scenario. Just when she thought she had a handle on it, things blew up. "Do you really think it's me they want?"

"Oh, they want you all right, really bad. This is the third time they've attempted to get you. What I don't know is why."

"Maybe they should find me then," she suggested suddenly.

He turned and looked at her. "You don't want that," he replied quietly.

"No, I don't want it," she agreed, "but, for whatever reason, they seem to think that I'm important. How else do we find out why?"

"Is there any chance that your friend Pamela may have led them to believe something about you?"

Leah shrugged. "In desperate times, I imagine Pamela might have done anything she could to save her life or her sister's life. Just think about what people do when they're up against the wall."

"Exactly," he murmured. "I just wonder what they could possibly want from you."

"Because, *otherwise*, I don't have anything to offer, is that what you're saying?"

He turned. "No, not at all, but they're going to pretty extreme lengths to get you, and that concerns me."

"It concerns me as well. I hate not knowing why." Just then her phone rang. She stared down at it almost hysterically, and then she answered it.

Immediately her boss called out, "What the hell is that noise?" he roared.

"We're under attack," she cried out. "Why are you calling?"

"My God," he replied, silent for a moment. "I was calling to update you on the daughter. She's missing."

"Of course she is. We suspected that she might have been in the vehicle we spotted, when her father collected coffee. Remember? I told you about my street cams search from earlier this morning."

"Why would he do that?"

"If she was in the vehicle with the kidnapper, then the father wouldn't pull anything in the coffee shop, would he?"

"Right. He would have gone in and gotten coffee, I suppose."

"Lachlan thinks it might have been a test or something," she noted. "I don't know. None of this makes any sense."

Just then, more rapid gunfire ripped through the air.

"Oh my God," Ron gasped. "I thought you were supposed to be safe."

"We were," she stated, "but we're on the move to a new location."

"Doesn't sound like that move was a very good idea."

"We had to do something," she noted. "Our place was compromised. Remember the front door blown down so the two gunmen could grab me?" She shook her head, worrying more and more about Ron.

"I know. I know." Ron hesitated before speaking again. "At least you have some of the best men looking after you."

"True," she agreed quietly. "Ron, do you have any idea why these hacker guys would be after me?" she asked.

"No, I was going to ask you that. I mean, if they're being as persistent as they are, it sounds like they're pretty serious about taking you in."

"Oh, they're serious all right," she noted, wanting to laugh hysterically. "But, if I had some idea about *why*, I would know more and would be better equipped to deal with this. Can you keep hunting down the vehicle following us from yesterday?"

"Yeah. No sign of it yet. Can you see who's after you now?"

"No, and I'm not allowed to raise my head," she replied.

Just then more shots were fired, and the windshield took another direct hit.

"I don't know how long the bulletproof glass will last," she noted, now worrying about yet another new thing.

"I'll talk to you when this is over," Ron said. "We're on it."

"Yeah, about time," she muttered.

"Hey …" After a momentary pause, he murmured, "I am really sorry about that."

"Let's just hope you get to apologize in person," she muttered, "because right now? It's looking pretty unlikely from my end."

"No, you'll make it," Ron argued. "Hang in there. I'll get back to you as soon as I can." And, with that, he hung up.

She stared down at the phone, shaking her head. "I know you guys were asking me if there is any reason for my boss Ron to have been compromised, but he sounded pretty shook up about hearing the gunfire."

"He may be shook up, but that doesn't mean he's upset enough to make me happy," Lachlan noted, as she looked over at him.

"And I suppose it's important that you are happy, *huh*?"

"No, maybe not," he admitted, "but it's damn important that I don't think it's him because otherwise I'll go to that office and rip him limb from limb, until I find out how he's involved."

"Let's just hope it's not him," she replied. The vehicle kept dodging and weaving, and she still couldn't see anything. "God, I don't even know what I'm supposed to do if I get picked up by one of these kidnappers."

"You give them everything that you need to in order to stay alive," Lachlan ordered, "because the bottom line is that we'll be on their tail, looking for you."

"Yeah, well, we haven't done so well figuring out anything about them so far."

"We're getting closer every day," he stated calmly. "So, if it does happen, just tell them what they want to know."

"I agree," Axel chipped in.

"Me too," Jonas added.

"If it comes down to that, get your ass out of there, if you can," Lachlan added. "Otherwise, just know that you're not alone."

She hated to feel like his words were prophetic, but they came so suddenly in response to this current gunfire that it made her heart skip a beat. She looked up at him to see his grim face surveying the area around them. "How come there are no sirens?" she asked.

"Probably because most people are still trying to keep their heads down, waiting for all this to be over," he explained. "We're also multiple blocks away from where this started."

She nodded. "I can understand that. Can I sit up now?"

"No!" Came a unified response from everybody in the vehicle.

She glared at them. "*Great.* How will you know if I recognize them?"

"You won't recognize them," Lachlan stated immediately.

"I might," she muttered.

"You won't," he repeated.

She threw up her hands. "Why is that?"

"Because they're not here. They're gone now."

"Shit," she said. "You know what? I hate to say it, but we really need to catch these guys, preferably before they kill anybody else."

"You mean, like you?" Lachlan asked, with a smile.

"Yeah, that would be nice," she muttered, "or I'll let you explain it to my mother."

"Have you spoken to her recently?"

She stared at him in shock. "Oh no. No, no, no." She shook her head adamantly. "You don't get to spring something like that on me."

"I'm not springing anything on you," he argued calmly.

"Yes, you are. Yes, you are," she snapped. "That's not fair."

He just looked at her, but she was already dialing. When her mom answered the phone, she muttered, "Oh, thank God."

Her mom was surprised by that greeting. "What's the matter?" she asked. "Are you in trouble again?"

"No! I'm not in trouble again," she replied. "I was just making sure that you were fine."

"Of course I'm fine," she snapped. "Is this important? I can't talk long, as I have company over."

"No, no, I guess it's not important." Leah stopped, immediately alarmed. "What company?"

"The Ladies Club, honey. You know we have our book club meetings."

"Right, sorry to disturb you." Then Leah hung up.

"Wow, what was that all about?" Lachlan asked.

"I disturbed her on her book club night," she explained. "Believe me. She's fine."

"That's a good thing," he replied.

"Then people really won't understand the relationship I have with my mother."

"Not great, I gather."

"It depends what you mean by *great*," she noted. "My mother is a unique soul."

"Aren't they all?" he asked, with laughter in his voice.

She sighed. "Some are a little more unique than others."

He nodded. "Oh, I get that—not an easy relationship, I presume."

"It's fine as long as I toe the line, don't get into trouble, and don't bother her," she explained.

"Ouch, all of that, *huh*?"

"All of that," she confirmed, with a nod. "But that's okay. I've since learned how to handle life with my mother."

"That's a good thing. It sounds like she's an interesting person and somebody who cares about you."

"She cares," she admitted. "It's just that her version of caring is very different from mine."

"I think that's a common complaint among children," he murmured. "With a lot of people in the world, it makes for a lot of unique relationships in the mix."

She looked at him sharply. "What about you? How is your relationship with your family?"

"Interesting," he noted, with a smile. "I try not to tell them very much about what I'm up to."

"That probably makes them happy," she replied, laughing.

"The less they know, the less they can get upset and worried about," he stated. "My dad is in law enforcement, so he has a pretty good idea, and he doesn't bother me with questions. As I said, the less he has to worry about, the better."

"I get that," she agreed. "I'm not even sure mine is in that category. It's more a case of the less she knows, the better on all things Leah."

"Got it." Lachlan nodded. "Lots of people are like that."

"They are," she noted, "and, by keeping her out of the loop, she's happier, and I'm happier."

He just smiled and acknowledged what she wasn't saying, which is the fact that her mom walked to her own drum, and that was just the way life was.

"She's a good person though," she added suddenly.

"Yep, I hear that," he murmured. "You don't have to feel guilty."

"And yet I do feel guilty." Leah groaned. "And I'll blame you for that."

He smirked and then shrugged. "You do whatever makes your heart happy."

"Does that mean I get to punch you too?"

"Would that make you happy?" he asked, turning to face her.

"No," she said, "that would just make me feel like an idiot."

He chuckled. "You are in a conundrum then, aren't you?"

"No, I'm not." She nodded with relief now that the vehicle moved normally again. "Did everybody survive?" she asked quietly.

"All of us did, … yes," Lachlan confirmed.

"Even Jonas?"

"Yeah." Lachlan nodded. "Why would you even doubt it?" he asked on a laugh.

"Because he's been fairly quiet so far."

"Yeah, but mostly due to the constraints of his job," he murmured.

"And all of that's just crap," she argued. "I mean, when you think about it, there's only so much that anybody can get blamed for."

"In a case like this, that's gone international, you can bet everybody is involved, and everybody is working hard at trying to keep people alive," Lachlan explained. "It's not a case of who's involved and who's not involved. It's a matter of tracking these guys down. The minute they crossed over from England to Germany, they changed their status in the criminal world."

"Which was not very wise of them," she noted. "Do you think they did that on purpose? It seems like they were asking MI6, Interpol, and various other local law enforcement agencies to all get involved."

Lachlan turned toward her and shrugged. "I'm not sure, but you're right. It wasn't very wise of them. Brought a whole new level of interest down on them, that has just followed them here to Germany."

"So why would they do that?" she asked, studying Jonas crouching in the back alongside her.

"Any idea?" Jonas asked, turning toward her.

She shrugged. "No, I just think that it's a really interesting problem."

"It is, and statistically it changed this case quite a bit, didn't it?"

"Sure," she agreed, "another reason it doesn't make sense to make it more international."

"Unless it was a spinoff," Axel suggested, "of something else."

She spun to look at him. "Meaning?"

"A splitting of partners perhaps? Maybe somebody was doing it for one reason, like the usual *power, sex, revenge.* Then another one decided to get rich quick. However, because there never seems to be enough money to satisfy the criminals in the world, they needed to do it over and over again, which caused problems, so they split off."

"That's an awful lot of guesswork," she noted, staring at the back of Axel's head.

"All we have at the moment is guesswork," Jonas replied quietly. "In case you hadn't noticed."

"Oh, I noticed." She gave him an eye roll. "I was just hoping we would have a little more in the way of actual facts at this point."

"We're getting there." Lachlan smiled and patted her knee.

"Promise?" she muttered.

"I do promise," he said, laughing. "We just need a little bit more time."

"It's frustrating," she admitted, "because it seems like everybody is involved, and yet there are too many factors. I mean, why so many banks? Why England? Why Germany?"

"All really good questions," Lachlan noted. "I think we need to delve into those a little bit more."

"I think it should require Jonas too," she stated. "I don't

know exactly how his role in all of this came about, but it sounds like the England part will play an important role here in Germany."

"I wonder why though," Lachlan murmured.

"I don't know. Again we don't have any information—or enough of it," she complained, "but, if we had an idea of who this group was who just shot at us, it might help. That means we need to ID those men who keep following us, not to mention the two who blew up the front door today."

At that, Lachlan's phone buzzed. He looked down at the text and smiled. "Tesla, with perfect timing as usual."

"What's she saying?"

"She's got an ID on the two men in the safe house."

"Both of them?" she asked in delight.

"Yep. They're both Americans, which is why she got the ID easier and faster, and look at that. … They were both military, now private."

"That explains some things," she said, "but not a whole lot." He looked at her as she shrugged. "I mean, that's how they ended up getting into the safe house fairly easily. Could have been special ops. Who knows?" she murmured. "But the best thing is that we have them."

"Which means that now we can dig deeper into their known associates," Axel added.

"Gosh, I would love to get into this hunt," she shared, "if I could only actually, you know, get to a computer."

Lachlan smiled. "I know you're quite pissed off about leaving all that computer equipment behind."

"You might have left it all behind, but I didn't. I kept the secured laptop and packed it with my things." He frowned at her; she shrugged. "I wouldn't take the chance of leaving it behind because I hadn't had an opportunity to clean that one off yet."

He nodded. "You can make whatever apologies you want to make later. We're just following orders."

"That's too damn bad," she muttered. "I'm really tired of taking orders when people aren't being very good about giving explanations."

"Haven't you noticed that's a very common thing with a lot of these outfits, especially governments?" he asked, with a smile.

"Maybe, but that doesn't mean I have to like it though." At that, he burst out laughing. She looked over at him. "How come you always have such a good attitude?" she asked.

"Is that a problem?"

"I don't know." She shrugged. "The jury is still out on that."

He shook his head and said, "Wow, lady, you are a tough person to please."

"Am I?" His words suddenly hit her, and she thought about it for a moment. "You know what? You're right. I probably am," she admitted, "and I'm sorry about that."

He stared at her for a moment. "Where did all that come from? What just happened?" he asked, "I'm not complaining, of course, but still."

"You probably should be though," she muttered, "because I have been difficult to get along with."

"I think you're driven to do something and to do your best at all times. Being new is never easy."

"No, it sure as hell isn't," she agreed. "But it's not as if I've had the opportunity to do anything different."

"Well, you do now."

"Maybe," she muttered. "Maybe if I look at other options, but this is what I wanted to do."

"And why is that? Do you know?"

She frowned and then shrugged, not wanting to delve too deeply into her motives. At least not right now.

LACHLAN KEPT A close eye on her and all around them after they got to their new location. This was an apartment in a pretty grungy area of town, but one they had worked with many times before, and, according to Jonas, it was tactically suitable at least. He wasn't talking about location or anything else in this part of the world, just that it was available. And, of course, Lachlan believed it because everybody had safe houses and other assets accessible to them all around the world, and they guarded those secrets very carefully.

In this case it was Jonas's choice because he had one available and ready. It was also much cleaner and higher-end than it appeared from the outside. Leah hadn't been impressed at all when they had first walked into the back door. But when they got into the actual apartment, she calmed right down. She now sat in the living room, staring off in the distance.

"Are you thinking about somebody specifically?" Lachlan asked quietly. "Or just spiraling?"

She looked over at him, and then shook her head. "My mind is spinning away on the details."

"I can have your laptop brought to you."

"You mean somebody's laptop," she noted. "I would very much like to go to the office."

He sat down beside her and took a careful look at her face. She didn't appear to be anything other than earnest. "Why?" he asked bluntly.

"Because I can have real access there. I don't have external access from here, and I don't trust any of the internet around here to actually get me in and out of where I need to go and to do it stealthily."

"You could ask Tesla."

"To access, yes, I could," she agreed, "but she won't necessarily know what to look for."

"Do you?" he asked bluntly.

She nodded slowly. "Yes, I just don't like what is in the back of my mind right now, and I need to have my equipment," she noted quietly.

"And here I thought you'd probably have the same level of equipment at your own place."

"You would have thought so," she agreed, "but I've gotten way too complacent about being at work. That'll have to change now."

"You mean, because of Pamela?"

She nodded. "Partly, yes."

"Are you sure?"

"Damn sure. Only partly." She looked over at him. "I get that you're looking for more information, but I don't have it to give you," she stated, "and, even if I did right now, I wouldn't share it. There's something in the back of my mind that I need to check out, but I need to have *all access* in order to do that. That means you need to get me back into my office, without me being seen."

His eyebrows shot up. This was the direct order he had been expecting all along. "I hear you. And when is it you expect me to get this done?"

"Right now, please," she stated, her tone cool, but her directive didn't leave him any doubt that she was serious.

"Even though it's not in your best interests?"

"I believe that it's in all of our best interests."

He thought about both what she'd said and what she hadn't said and then took a guess. "You think somebody at your office is involved?" Her eyes widened at that. He shrugged. "I don't have to be a hacker to see the lay of the land, you know?"

"We already know there's a hacker," she noted.

"And that was Pamela?"

"But Pamela was low-level, and she had limited access," she added.

"So they want you for something specific, for some greater access."

"I really don't get that part."

"Does Tesla have any ideas?"

"I haven't asked her," she admitted. "And again, communication is spotty from here, and I don't want too much written down."

"Got it," he noted. "Do you have any reason to suspect anyone in particular?"

She shook her head. "No, it's really just instincts at this point."

He laughed.

"Which is something I suppose you think is foolish?" she asked.

He immediately shook his head. "No, that's not what I think at all." He stated simply, "Instincts have saved our lives more than a few times." She looked at him curiously, and he shrugged. "I think we slowly gain an inner awareness of when we're in danger and when we're not," he murmured. "We're not always right, and sometimes fear plays a bigger part in that than anything, but, if you tell me that you think you have something that you need to check out, then I'll make that happen," he murmured.

She smiled brilliantly. "So do you want to do that right now?" she asked, nudging him.

He laughed. "Nothing about you is pushy, is there?"

"I try not to be," she said, with a wince. "I tend to be direct, and I'm definitely not in my element in this job. It is new for me, which is partly why I think Tesla wanted you guys over here. Which is foolish because I'm supposed to be training you, not you guys helping me."

"Hey, it is what it is," he noted. "Things took a turn, and that's just life. Besides, we'll stay afterward and get the training anyway."

At that, she grinned. "Sounds good to me." She nodded, showing her palms. "This was a six-month stint, as far as I knew. But there was also a suggestion of this being a test to bigger things, if all goes well. And if that's what I want."

"But if you're stirring up trouble while you're here …"

"I haven't been," she stated calmly. "I was trying to stay calm and quiet, running below the radar, you know?"

"Any reason?"

"Sometimes people don't really like my methodology," she explained, "and I can get into trouble for coloring outside of the lines."

"Do you care?"

She laughed at that. "You know what? Most of the time I don't care at all, but this is a new venture for me, and I was trying to get along."

"And now?"

"Now I think I might have been put over here without people really realizing that I would actually see something," she offered. "I don't know that for sure or if it's just a coincidence. I just don't know."

"Tell me something," Lachlan stated. "Having listened to what you just said, have you been looking at something other than your regular day-to-day stuff?"

She stared at him. "Did I just say that?" she asked.

"I'm reading between the lines."

"It might be better if you didn't read between the lines," she said instantly.

"Too late," he stated. When she glared at him, he smiled back at her. "Listen. It's just taking us longer to work through this, so why don't you just come clean?"

"I can't just *come clean*," she argued, "but there were a few anomalies. And I'm not terribly happy with those anomalies now, after these last couple days."

"Yeah, seeing all that's happened, I would think so."

Just then Axel and Jonas came inside, after some reconnaissance outside. Lachlan walked over to join them and explained what she wanted to do. With eyebrows raised, Jonas immediately shook his head. "We finally just got to a place where she's safe, and now she wants to leave again?"

Lachlan nodded and didn't even bother trying to explain it any further than that. It was already a done deal in his mind, and, if Jonas didn't like it, that was too bad.

Axel seemed to realize that they were well past the point of even discussing it. He looked over at Lachlan. "When?"

"Now," he replied quietly.

Axel immediately turned and opened the door, motioning them through. "Let's go then."

And, with that, Lachlan walked over to her and reached out a hand. She placed hers in it, and he led her back down to the garage.

CHAPTER 10

W HEN LEAH WALKED into her office, Markus didn't even show surprise. So somebody had already told him that they were coming. He just gave her a hard nod, his gaze searching the area, then connecting with the men behind her and moving on.

Her boss came running out of his office. "I didn't know you were coming," he greeted her happily.

She smiled at him. "I needed to come in to do some work. I was going a little squirrely, you know?"

"Of course, of course," he replied, rubbing his hands together. "And you know there's never any shortage of work here. I'm so happy you are safe."

She laughed. "There's never any shortage of work anywhere," she noted, with a sigh. "As for being safe, the jury is still out."

He nodded again. "I have a meeting in ten," he said, looking at his watch, "but, if you'd given me some warning, I could have rescheduled."

"That's fine." She waved her hand. "I've got a bunch of stuff to check, and then, when I get clear of all that, if you're back again, we can meet up."

"Perfect." Ron looked at the men behind her. "Markus here has been very diligent," he noted. "He won't let any of us do anything really."

"That's important for everybody's safety," she noted.

"I know. After Pamela especially," he admitted. "We're all shocked at her death."

Leah wondered if Ron had passed on the news about what Pamela had been caught up in, thinking she wouldn't really blame him if he hadn't. It's hard enough to do what they were doing without facing that kind of betrayal. She herself didn't judge Pamela's actions—especially when Leah knew that Pamela's only living relative had been threatened.

What was anybody supposed to do in a situation like that? It just seemed way too easy for these bad guys to get at people though, which was another bothersome point. How would they have even found Pamela? That was definitely something that needed to be answered, yet Leah knew it could be as simple as talking with somebody who used to know Pamela or who had found out where she was working now.

A simple update on social media could often be blamed for that kind of crap too.

People were encouraged not to say much online, and, even if they didn't, they gave just enough details that anybody with half a brain and some decent skills on the internet could find out more. It was frustrating because it made Leah's job that much harder at the same time.

As she moved toward her office, Lachlan stayed at her side. "Will you be my shadow all day?"

"Yep, and tomorrow," he replied cheerfully. "And maybe the day after that too."

"Great," she muttered. "That can't be much fun."

"It's actually delightful," he admitted, "just like you."

She rolled her eyes at that. "You aren't getting anywhere using that smooth talk on me," she muttered.

"Not trying to," he stated. "I mean it. I've enjoyed spending time with you."

She stared at him. "Don't tell Tesla and Mason that. We'll never hear the end of it."

He burst out laughing. "Please tell me that you wouldn't refuse to go out with me just because of that whole matchmaking reason," he noted.

She stared at him. "What? Are you really asking me out on a date?"

"It's an interesting question, isn't it?" he asked. "I mean, when I came over to Germany, I had been tipped off to the whole matchmaking idea, yet it was the last thing on my mind to even look at you in that way." He shrugged. "Just something about you hits the right note."

"*Great*," she murmured, "so you'll just play me like an instrument then."

"No," he stated, with a big grin. "Yet that does bring up some interesting ideas." He waggled his eyebrows.

She rolled her eyes, as she sat down at her computer and quickly logged in. Once in, she checked to ensure nobody had had access to her computer, and, with a sigh of relief, she sat back.

"What was that for?" he asked.

She looked over at him, then motioned at the door. He closed it and then pulled something from his pocket and walked around her room.

"Are you sweeping it?" she asked in a hushed whisper.

He nodded. "Markus already did. I'm just checking it out at one extra level."

"Interesting," she murmured. "Is it clear?"

"It's clear," he stated. "Were you expecting it to be clear?"

"I wasn't expecting you to even check," she admitted, "so I don't know what to say. But now that it's clear, I feel much better."

"Right." Lachlan smiled. "It's not just about electronics, and the old technology still has an awful lot to offer."

"I generally forget about it," she said. "We live in such an internet age now that it's easy to forget that people can do so many other tricks that have nothing to do with the internet."

"All the more reason to take advantage of both," he noted.

"And why wouldn't they? Is that what you mean?"

"Yeah, I mean, most people aren't looking beyond the net anymore," he replied quietly. "Not only are they not looking for it, a lot of them, unless they're in the field, don't even have any access or understanding of how any of this older stuff works."

"Which then makes it an advantage for us, doesn't it?"

"Absolutely it does," he agreed, with a nod. "And anything we can do to our benefit is huge."

"I guess," she murmured. "I don't even think of it that way anymore."

"That's because you spend so much time on your computer," he explained. "You've got to get out of the office and see the real world more."

She snorted at that. "Like you guys had me out of the office into the real world yesterday and today? How fun was that?"

"When we're done here, we will have fun," he stated.

She nodded. "Right, that sounds like a perfect answer." But her head was already down, and she went through the history on her computer. Then she checked some of the spider bots that she'd built to also track movements. It was instinctive on her part to track the movements of those around her.

The trouble was, she hadn't checked it lately. So, even though she had a tracking mechanism set up in the system, once she hadn't found any kind of problems in the initial stages of her job, she hadn't bothered checking up on it anymore, hadn't built in any alerts to let her know if somebody was delving into databases that they weren't supposed to be in.

"Shit." She scrubbed her face, seeing that people had definitely been going through some of the databases that weren't supposed to be allowed in. Then, not knowing who it was, she set off to find out.

When her phone buzzed, it was Tesla, and she texted just a user name.

Of course Tesla was in the system, monitoring any movement. **Interesting**, Leah responded. **You chose my boss.**

Tesla sent a happy face and a little thumbs-up.

Leah shook her head at that. Why was Tesla logging in under her boss' name? Leah had already considered Ron as potentially being part of this, but he wasn't a great target. He was also, well, she hated to say it, but he wasn't really the type to have ambitions.

He had his government job in a field that he was quite happy with, then managed to make a promotion after a decade of being here, and even now looked like he was ready to just stay until he retired. He didn't put out any more effort than was required, as she had seen firsthand lately, which wasn't such a surprise after all.

Watching where Tesla had gone and checking into the history and background in Ron's own movements, she nodded. "I guess that makes sense," she mumbled to herself. But, if Tesla had logged in, who else had? She quickly texted her friend that same question.

I didn't see anybody, Tesla texted. **But his log-in, his password, all from his desk, were the points of entry. The problem that I see is that they were all during non-work hours.**

Leah winced at that, so she picked up her phone and quickly called Tesla. "So you're thinking he looks good for this?"

"He looks good, but it's almost too easy."

"Yeah, that's why I wasn't too sure about even going in that direction because it seemed like a waste of time."

"And I get that," Tesla noted. "I've just seen way-too-many people who are too good at this who make it look like they're being stupid and not somebody worth looking at."

"Which is also scary," Leah noted. "Again it's a matter of staying the course and continuously checking to make sure that we upturn every rock in our pathway."

"If you have somebody else that you're considering, let me know."

"Not really," Leah admitted. "I'm sure you've checked every person who works in the office. I have."

Tesla added, "There are a couple questions that I do have about a few of them."

"Fire away," Leah replied.

As Tesla started with one name, Leah quickly looked into their individual case history. "I don't think his child's death is an issue, is it? According to the medical records, he died of SIDS, so I'm thinking not," Leah replied.

"But he was also having trouble getting the doctors to look at him," Tesla noted.

"Also interesting."

"Why?" Tesla asked Leah.

"Medical here is free."

"Not for American citizens."

"I guess then it's what, US medical?"

"Yes, on the military bases."

"*Hmm*, that's interesting," Leah murmured. "I'm sure in some cases they manage to get private care."

"In this one, he paid a large amount of money to get answers."

"And yet they were answers after the fact."

"Yes," Tesla agreed, her voice low. "Almost as if expecting it to have been something else."

"Right," she murmured. "So am I supposed to go talk to him?"

"I wouldn't at this point," Tesla suggested. "Where's your boss right now?"

"He's in a meeting. Why?"

"Take a look at his log-in."

At that, Leah quickly logged out, then using the same program as Tesla, she logged in to see who was on the system. And, sure enough, her boss was on the system. "Could he be accessing it from the meeting?" she wondered out loud.

"It's possible, or somebody else is utilizing it."

"But you're saying, … and the bot says, it's coming from his computer."

"I know," she stated. "Can you get up and walk past that office?"

"Yeah, I'm on my way." Leah bolted to her feet, and, at a relatively unhurried pace for her, she walked out of her office, with Lachlan quietly at her side. Obviously having picked up some of what was going on, he stayed close, as she headed toward Ron's office.

When she got there, she noted the room was empty. "Fascinating," she murmured. She had turned back toward her office when one of the women called out.

"He's gone to a meeting but isn't back yet."

Leah lifted a hand in acknowledgment, then detoured to the coffeepot to pour herself a healthy mugful and one for Lachlan. She handed him his and, without saying another word to anybody, headed back to her office.

He immediately turned on the bug finder as soon as they got in again. She stared at it, then him. "It's not on my radar to check that every time."

"That's why I'm here," he stated. "It'll also scramble anybody if they try to listen in."

She took a deep breath, then nodded.

"So you want to explain what's going on?" She told him what they'd just found. His eyebrows shot up. "So they have a way to make it look like what they're doing is coming from his office?"

"Exactly," she replied. "And that in itself is fascinating because even *I* don't know how to do that."

"But you know how to hide your tracks?"

"Of course." She nodded. "However, I can't make it look like it's coming from a specific IP. Particularly with the firewalls that we have here."

"Also interesting."

At that, Markus knocked on the door and stepped inside. She looked up at him, then frowned. "We've got a problem."

"Yep, we sure do," Markus agreed.

She looked at him and said, "You first."

He frowned and then nodded. "Your boss was due at a meeting and didn't show up."

She winced at that. "Seriously? Do we know where he is?"

"Not at this point in time," he stated. "I've been asked if you do."

"Who even knows I'm here?" she asked.

"Apparently news travels fast."

She thought about that and suggested, "I did log in, so security would know for sure."

"And, if Ron's meeting was in this building, they have to be wondering just where he is."

"They should have camera access everywhere." She rubbed her temples before working her keyboard, backtracking to the cam feed of her in Ron's office. She watched him online as he exited his office and headed to the elevator. When she fast-forwarded to check each of the floors, the elevator didn't open up on any of them; hence she didn't see him actually get off. "I'm not seeing him exit," she noted quietly. "Or heading to the garage level."

"Security is looking at the garage level, and they're also worried about a kidnapping."

"We're all worried about everything," she admitted. "Particularly after Pamela."

"Exactly," Markus murmured.

Looking up at him, she stated, "Have security put out a small alarm, a quiet one. If he's just gone home or if he's in a bathroom somewhere, I don't want to raise the full alarm and institute a full lockdown. But, if he's in trouble, we need to know."

"And what if he's absconding because he saw your army? Would he make a run for it?"

"In that case, we also need to know," she stated. "He's not stupid. He has a long history of this kind of work, and, if he's involved, then he'll do everything he can to hide his tracks. But it would be a little too obvious right now."

"Unless he was already set to go," Lachlan added quietly.

"I know. I know." She typed away at her keyboard. "This is another security camera."

"Can you see him?"

"He's down on the basement level."

They immediately crowded around behind her, and she pointed at her screen. "This was fifteen minutes ago." They saw him rushing down a long hallway.

"Exactly where is that?" Markus asked, frowning.

Leah pulled up the related schematics to show him. "This building has two basements. This is the bottom one."

"I'll take that floor," he said. "If he's down there, I'll find him."

"It's also been fifteen minutes," she told Markus, "so Ron could have already moved on, but I'll keep hunting to see where he goes." Then just like that, Ron disappeared from the screen. "And that's as far as the cameras actually cover," she noted, as the two men looked at each other, and then Markus took off.

"Should he go alone?" she asked anxiously, turning to look at Lachlan.

"He'll meet up with Axel. Jonas is standing guard outside."

"Somebody needs to tell Jonas that it's possible Ron is running."

"Already did." Lachlan smiled. "Don't worry. We've got this."

"I hope so." She stared at her screen. "I would find it

very hard to imagine that Ron could be involved."

"Even after seeing that?"

She nodded. "Unless …" She frowned. "His wife is an invalid. If his wife has been taken, all bets are off."

"As you well know that's all too possible," he noted. "I'll find out."

And, with that, he stepped away, his phone ready, already dialing.

WITH NO ANSWER at Ron's house, not even the invalid wife answering herself, Lachlan put out the call to Jonas. "Hey, we've got Ron's wife, an invalid, not answering the phone. This Ron guy is skulking down around the lowest level of this building," he explained.

"Where do they live?"

"Within walking distance."

"Give me the address," Jonas said. "I'll walk over and check it out. Where is Markus? Axel just headed out to help him with something."

"Markus was headed downstairs to track Leah's boss through the building. Axel will meet him, but, if you end up needing help, check in with them. I'm staying to keep an eye on Leah."

"Not an issue," Jonas noted, and, with that, he hung up.

Lachlan stopped and stared through the privacy blinds on the inner windows of Leah's office into the small bullpen area where everybody else studiously kept their heads down. Almost too studiously. He frowned at that. "Could anybody else be involved? Like the entire department?"

"What would be the benefit of that?"

Nothing. It would be too many people, too many eyes

and ears to keep track of. The fact that Pamela and possibly Ron were involved was already too many in an office this size. And yet the *why* was the part that really mystified Lachlan. The *why* was what they needed answered. Lachlan turned toward Leah. "This isn't making sense."

"I know," she murmured. "I don't understand why."

"That's what I was thinking. These guys have got to be looking for something else." Just then his phone buzzed. He pulled it out to hear Mason on the other end.

"Another bank manager has been taken, and this one's in England again."

"You know what?" Lachlan said quietly. "I think we have two factions going on. Likely a split within the original group, and now we've got somebody in England who's pulling their own games, while someone here in Germany is running the same op but different."

"That's been tossed out as an option," Mason murmured.

Lachlan added, "We're trying to get anything that will confirm it. Meanwhile, have you found any known associates of those two gunmen who bombed their way into our first safe house?"

"Yes, and one of them is alive in England. Another has popped up, floating dead in the Thames."

"Right, so I'm back to thinking we've got split factions," Lachlan repeated. "The question is, what do the ones here in Germany want, and what are the ones over there in England after?"

"I think the ones over there want money and a way to disappear," Mason suggested. "The ones there in Germany with you are after something completely different."

"And that would explain why the factions have split."

"Yes, it would, but it's still not giving us any connection between the two groups," Mason noted.

"The boss here has just skedaddled out from underneath the building. As soon as Leah came in to work, he booked it, claiming he had a meeting to attend and would talk to her in a few minutes. When he was out of sight, instead of going to the meeting, he hit the basement floors."

"Tesla was just telling me," Mason noted.

"Markus is on the hunt."

"Okay, while it's good that things are breaking apart, they'll have to break a whole lot faster and a whole lot cleaner for us to get fully on to them."

"You've got good men on it," Lachlan noted. "So just stand by."

"Yeah, we got that happening," Mason agreed. "And don't let your eyes off Leah."

"I'm not," Lachlan stated, turning immediately to confirm she still sat here at her computer. "I know she's struggling to get behind what's going on, but what we can't figure out is Ron's motive yet. Whether it is personal or if maybe the bad guys are after her and her boss. Maybe the boss is going after the bad guys because they have his invalid wife. It could be anything as simple as revenge or just his emotions out of control. On the financial side, however, even about power, Leah's the rising star within the department, and Ron could worry she'll be after his job or something."

"Right, but to hit a bank like this? ... That doesn't sound like anything Ron would mastermind. And we're pulling his full history."

"I saw that," Lachlan replied. "I already took a look at everybody in the office. The one thing that struck me about

Ron's history was that it was squeaky clean. It's too good."

"Meaning?" Mason asked.

"I just feel like somebody went in and doctored it."

"It's possible, but to have had the access—"

"Unless he did it himself. He's been in this department for many years," he murmured. "It's quite possible that, over time, he cleaned it up and added to it."

"And what would that do?"

"Well, just think about it," he stated. "Who is it that he's after? What is he after and why?"

"And you said he's got an invalid wife?"

"Yes, and I'm looking into her history too."

"I'll put Tesla on that as well," he replied. "We all need answers, and we need them damn fast. But now that you mentioned Ron's invalid wife, I'm just wondering what put her in that state."

"Good point. Let me see." He hung up and walked over to Leah. In a low tone, he asked, "The invalid wife, how did that happen?"

She looked up and punched open one of the files. "This file doesn't say very much about it. Just that there was a car accident."

"And who was driving?"

"Hang on." She kept clicking away on the keys, getting information from the database. "It was a hit-and-run, and nobody was charged."

"So, if Ron had any idea of who'd done it, is there any way he would do something like this to get back at them?"

"That makes no sense," she noted. "It doesn't sound like he's getting anything, and he has nobody he knows potentially to blame."

"But maybe he does. Maybe he has a good idea but

knows that there's no way that he'll get justice."

She stared at him. "And that would mean we're talking about political assistance or in some way somebody influential inside this building itself? Even so, it's not like Ron's getting anything in return."

Lachlan shook his head. "And yet he's probably getting insurance money, or was at least, but that could already be exhausted, so maybe she needs more care than Ron can actually get for her. Maybe she's declining and needs some kind of treatment or surgery that's not covered."

"I'm pulling her medical records," Leah said immediately, and it took her two minutes. He hated to admit he was timing her, but she was damn fast.

"Okay she's ... Oh, shit." And she stopped to look at the file closely. "Yeah, she's definitely declining, and she has developed cancer. Ron's wife needs special treatment." Leah quickly read through the file, then shook her head and sagged before continuing. "According to her doctors, no such treatment is available in Germany. She would have to go for an experimental treatment. This says she mentioned Mexico to her doctor. But Ron's bank account is healthy, and he could definitely afford it, if that's what he chose."

"But is his bank account really that flush, or is it just made to look that way, so nobody thinks that he has a reason to go and do something like this?"

She stared at him and immediately started punching through the banking sites. "You're not allowed to watch," she stated.

"I don't know anything," he replied, "just give me answers."

She chuckled. "This is why I got into trouble in the first place."

"Hey, you're doing an investigation into somebody who's out there killing people."

"It's the killing that I don't get," she murmured.

"I'm wondering if that isn't the other faction's MO," he suggested.

"Ron has a brother," she said, suddenly looking up.

"Not according to his files," Lachlan noted in surprise.

"Maybe not, but I did hear him talk about it once. When I asked him about his brother, he told me that his brother died a long time ago."

At that, Lachlan immediately phoned Mason and let him know. "I think we may be onto something here."

"What is it?"

"Leah's checking out Ron's bank accounts to see if substantial money is actually there or if it's a cover."

"Hard to make it look like money is there if it's not," Mason noted cautiously. "At least to the hackers among us."

"I know. I'm not sure what's going on there. But Leah found Ron has a brother, supposedly dead. She'll look further into each."

With that, Lachlan hung up again, then sat down and waited, his fingers tapping on the armrest of the chair. He'd take action any day over sitting here and waiting for other people. But his job was to look after her, and, if he sat down and got hung up on some internet research of his own, no way would she remain his primary focus.

"Holy shit!" She looked at him and said, "His bank account is empty."

"What do you mean empty?"

"Empty, as in zero dollars. There's nothing in it."

He stared at her in shock. "As in, he's leaving the country and had to empty his bank account?"

"It was emptied yesterday," she added quietly.

"Interesting," he murmured. "Did somebody take that money? Did somebody …" He stopped.

"It was withdrawn in a wire transfer." She quickly clicked through. "That's interesting. It went to the Cayman Islands."

"And was it transferred to him? That's the main question now."

"I don't have access to that information," she noted. "It's a numbered account, and I can't easily get anything that'll tell us that."

"Damn, so either he is making plans to jump ship or he had to pay somebody for something under the table."

"Possibly the treatment for his wife or to take out somebody he doesn't like," she suggested quietly.

He stared at her. "And it's also possible that this other faction gave him a bunch of money, and it went to the wrong account. And that could be to pay him for services or to just get him in trouble."

"Which is possible because it looked like a ton of money was in there, as in four million dollars, and now it's all gone."

"But, of course, that also looks like some crazy banking error. It went in, and it went out."

"Yes," she agreed. "That's exactly what it looks like."

"Or he moved it in, then moved it out, and that was his share from something—or money laundering. Who the hell knows at this point?"

"Again it's all speculation," she noted. "It could be anything. I do know that everything I've ever heard from him is that he really loved his wife."

"And yet you just used past tense."

She winced. "I also know that having somebody like that in your life, even when you love them, can be a burden."

"And maybe it's a burden he was ready to let go of," he noted quietly.

"I have to wonder about that too," she agreed, "though it makes me sick."

"Maybe this was his chance at a whole new life," he suggested.

"I would hate him for it," she stated. "How about his poor wife, who is bedridden and just hoping that her husband is coming home to relieve the length of her days and to make her life worth living, only to find out that he's booked it and taken all the money with him. That will put her on government support. She is an American citizen though, and maybe that could be part of his solution. I don't know what to think. Anything from Jonas?"

"No, but he hasn't had a chance to get anything on this angle yet."

She was grasping at straws. He knew it. She knew it, and yet he knew they were on the right track. "So, somebody, somehow is doing something that involves Ron, which is what we need to know. Now we have to find out if he's the bottom line or if there's more behind it."

"There's more behind it," she stated. "Somebody set this up, and they set it up a long time ago. The question is, who is doing it? And what is the end game that justifies all these deaths?"

CHAPTER 11

LEAH GOT UP and headed to join Lachlan, who had poured another coffee for each of them and was walking toward her. She reached out and accepted the cup from him. "Can we stand outside for a bit?" she asked. "I could use some fresh air."

"Absolutely. Do you have a special place?"

"A little balcony is out here." She led the way, and, as they stepped outside, she lifted her face to the sky and took a deep breath.

"All right, Leah. Let's hear it. What's going on in that head of yours?"

"You mean, the head that's about to explode? It's Ron. His history is too clean. His bank account is too clean. It all looks as if it's been doctored, but I'm not sure it was done by him."

"Go on," Lachlan said, enjoying watching her mind work.

"You see? I've known his work. I know what it's like to work with him. And honestly I don't think he's smart enough—or driven enough—to have done this. And I don't think he's clever enough to have written this code. But what I do think is that somebody is setting him up."

"Interesting," Lachlan replied. "Keep talking."

She shrugged. "I can't prove any of it yet. I haven't necessarily seen this same person's coding signature before, but it's very similar to Ron's." Then she stopped and shook her head. "This may sound crazy, I know, but I think it's *too* similar."

He stared. "Meaning that somebody is deliberately making it look like Ron has doctored his own history, put the money into his own bank account, and then immediately removed it."

She nodded. "Yes, I think that's exactly what's happening."

"But why?"

"I don't know, but I think it's also important to understand that Ron has been the one leading the task force on this banking investigation."

"So, it's making him look like an idiot?"

"Yes, and I don't know that he got all the information on these related cases," she noted. "I've just been looking at his emails, and he's missing a bunch of stuff. Remember when Markus got really angry at him? Apparently, at that point in time, and I know because I went back and checked, Ron sent off a whole series of furious emails, trying to figure out why he wasn't kept in the loop. So that makes you wonder if he's not being set up as incompetent as well. He's certainly being set up. I just don't know how or why. Or what the endgame is."

"Considering that it makes him look like he's an idiot, an incompetent fool who isn't doing anything in the midst of a crime wave, and that he's involved for personal gain, then jail and/or death could be the end result."

"So who would care enough to do all that to him?" she asked. "That was my first thought, and then I went in another direction." She took a deep breath. "I don't know if it's right or wrong." She then winced. "And unfortunately I don't think we'll find out ourselves."

"Why not?" he asked. "Explain."

"I went back to his wife's car accident. It was a hit-and-run. There was an investigation, and absolutely no leads were found. Nothing. So everything basically got closed or was made to look like it got closed, and, at the end of the day, nobody was charged or even suspected."

Lachlan shook his head. "Or simply a one-car accident?"

"Could be for all we know. He's been paying for her medical expenses, and, when he didn't have money, from what I could see, he got assistance from somewhere else."

"And you can't track where it came from?"

"No. Back to those numbered bank accounts again, but somebody cared enough to help him out."

"Or," Lachlan suggested, "somebody cared enough about *her*."

She nodded, her gaze studying him. "Yes, and you're picking up the exact same thing that I was afraid of."

"So who loves her enough to help Ron out enough to help her?"

"And again, that's another part of the problem," she noted. "I can't find any names, and I don't have any way to know who is involved, in either the accident itself or in the added money to help care for her."

"Jonas didn't find anything over at Ron's house, by the way. The place was locked up tight, no answer at the door. You'd think if she were there, someone would be with her if she's that bad off physically. Or she could answer the phone at least."

"I wonder if she's in a facility or something?"

"Could be, and that would cost an awful lot too, which

supports the theory that her care is beyond Ron's means."

"Yeah, I just wonder …"

"Wonder what? Do you have a suspicion?"

She nodded, took another deep breath. "I do have a suspicion, but I don't have anything to back it up."

"Speak up," he said. "We're just tossing out ideas anyway."

"I'm wondering if it is someone in her family."

LACHLAN STARED AT Leah for a few long moments and thought about everything she'd said. Then slowly he nodded. "That's possible. I mean, certainly someone in the family helping with medical expenses makes sense. I don't know why they would additionally try to make it look like Ron was incompetent or was involved in this whole thing with the hackers and their bank hits. Or maybe Ron *is* involved—or was to begin with—but they didn't want to bring Ron in on that level because it would expose them as well." Slowly nodding, Lachlan continued. "Criminals can't handle any additional controversy or publicity that could lead to their capture."

"Exactly," she agreed. "And, if Ron's not involved, I'm afraid somebody in the family is making it look like he is."

"Do you know if anybody associated with their family has that level of hacking skill? That stuff with his account is pretty specialized."

"I don't know," she replied. "I'm still researching that angle."

"It sounds to me like that needs to be boosted to the top priority."

"And I get that," she noted, "but it's not a very fast process."

"No? Let's look from another angle then. What's does his father-in-law do?"

She frowned. "He's some sort of diplomat."

"Ah," Lachlan said. "*Bingo.*"

"At least on the helping out part, that would make sense."

"Not to mention the part about avoiding publicity. Give me a name, and I'll get somebody to contact him."

"Good luck with that. As far as I know, he's not even in the country."

"Doesn't have to be really. A simple phone call can be done from anywhere."

When she gave him the name, he frowned. "I've heard this name before." He was quiet for a moment, then said, "Wonder who I can ask about this guy."

"Definitely ask Mason," she suggested. "Or maybe Jonas."

"Jonas would be a good one." Lachlan pulled out his phone, and, when Jonas answered, he asked, "Do you know of a Michael Danby?"

"Sure. Why?"

"You know him?"

"I know somebody who knows him," he clarified. "Just tell me what you need."

Lachlan quickly filled him in, then he turned and hung up. "Jonas has somebody who can call him directly."

"Right, so let's not do anything officially," she noted in a wry tone. "Not until we know if he's involved, and then it'll be official enough." She smiled. "And another thing, not implying you're sexist at all," she teased, "but you didn't ask about the mother-in-law. You know? The diplomat's wife."

He stared at her for a moment, then nodded slowly. "You are right. So tell me. What does she do?"

"She runs a big company in England," she replied. "A finance company of some sort, but I'm not exactly sure. I do have the name of it though."

"Send that to me too."

She pulled out her phone, delved into her emails and the notes that she'd written down, and sent it to him.

"Good enough," he said, as he studied it. "We'll see if there's anything in her history."

"I don't know that these people would do anything to hurt Ron, but—"

"At this stage in the investigation, we're looking at anything and everything," he stated. "Let's not feel bad about doing our job."

"No," she replied, "yet somehow I do."

"Not if it helps us get to the right conclusion," he noted quietly, and, with that, she had to be happy.

CHAPTER 12

A NEW FEELING of excitement buzzed as everybody gathered more information. She could only hope that it would unearth something important. She was also deliberately keeping her office staff out of it and everything that they had for updates. She wasn't sure who was involved and who wasn't, but what she really wanted was to find her boss and to figure out what the hell was going on.

As she went toward the elevators—hours after coming in, tired and stressed, but feeling like they actually had some breakthroughs going on—Lachlan stated, "Markus and Axel are still trying to track Ron down."

"Unbelievable. Do they need your help? I wouldn't mind taking a look at the basement levels myself," she added, after a moment.

"We can," he offered. "I don't know if you know the building well."

"No, I don't, not at all," she admitted. "But, if he went down there, he had to have a reason."

"We suspect another exit is there somewhere."

"You mean, like underground tunnels or something?"

"There could easily be service tunnels and the sewers of course."

"Maybe." She frowned. "Doesn't seem like Ron's kind of thing."

"But you don't know what he's having to do either."

She nodded and joined him as they took the elevator down as far as it went and then headed to the stairs. "It's so odd to even think how much of the world, as we know it, has another complete world underneath it."

"You know England is full of that kind of stuff."

"I know." She nodded. "I've half expected to be hauled over there as it is."

And the words had barely left her mouth when another voice popped in and said, "That's a good thing because that's exactly where you're heading."

She froze and turned to look at Lachlan. A muscle twitched at the corner of his jaw, and she saw he was furious. She slowly turned further to the new voice. "I'm sorry?"

"You heard me," one of the two men said. Neither one wore a mask, which caused more alarm than anything. As she stared at the guy who was the spokesman, she asked, "Do I know you?"

"Nope, you don't," he replied. "Not at all."

"So then why are you after me?" she asked.

They both had handguns. "It's got nothing to do with us," he told her. "We're just the delivery guys."

"And the package is you," the other one piped up. "What about him?" he asked the first guy, pointing his gun at Lachlan.

"He's disposable. Just trash the guy," he stated, immediately lifting his handgun and cocking it in their direction.

She sucked in her breath. "I wouldn't take to that very kindly," she murmured.

"Don't really give a shit." That was his instant response.

Her response was to distract him and to step in front of Lachlan. "So you'll just kidnap me and take me to England?

That makes no sense. I have nothing to do with anything."

"We don't think it makes any sense either, but, hey, orders are orders."

She nodded slowly. "If you say so."

"I do, but, if you'll be good, we'll take him along with us. Although from the looks of him, he'll be trouble."

"I'll be a handful of trouble if you *don't* bring him," she declared.

He laughed out loud at that. "I do like to see self-confidence." He chuckled. "I mean, I know you're about as dangerous as a butterfly, but hey."

"You don't know any such thing," she replied hotly.

The gunman who seemed to be in charge laughed. "Look at that. I think I struck a nerve. Did I insult you, milady?" he asked in a mocking tone.

She glared at him. "Are you serious about going to England?"

"Nope, not right now," he noted. "Only if they decide to keep you," he added a moment later.

She winced at that. "Oh, *great.*"

He motioned at her with his handgun. "Turn around and keep walking."

She slowly turned around and reached out a hand and Lachlan grabbed onto hers. The two of them walked forward.

"Now, isn't that nice?" the head gunman teased. "You've given us leverage to do exactly what we want you to do."

She continued talking, hoping to give Lachlan further cover. "If you're part of the lovely little banking heist that's been going on," she stated, "you could use somebody like him. No brains, but muscles he has in abundance."

"Maybe," the head guy admitted. "On the other hand,

we don't need brawn. If you haven't figured it out, we aren't killing the people we kidnap."

"No, you're killing somebody close to them."

"Yep, it works better that way. We just use the leverage that we have and manage to make everything work out. It's amazing what someone will do for the person they love."

"Maybe." Her fingers gripped Lachlan's hand tight. "But sometimes people just don't want to let assholes, like you, have the upper hand."

He burst out laughing again. "I like her," he told his gun-toting buddy. "Too bad it looks like you will be trouble too. So we'll have to kill both of you."

"So you *are* killing people you kidnap?" she snapped, pointing out his lie. Hoping this hadn't already happened before.

The head guy shrugged. "We don't plan on it, but it sometimes happens, you know?"

"Yeah, too bad," she muttered. Of course they wouldn't care. Nobody cared. This was all about them doing whatever the hell they had to for plans that didn't account for anyone else. "Besides, you guys are no longer attacking banks here."

"Says you. Remember? A bank manager is missing," the other man stated.

"Yeah," she said, "I do remember ... but—"

"But what?" he asked in an aggressive tone. "What do you know?"

"Probably nothing." She shrugged. "I just ... I get the feeling that there's been some split in upper management."

"There has been," he agreed, "but that was always in-tended."

"Right," she said, mentally chalking up one point for her. "It's too bad though."

"No, it's not too bad at all," he argued. "You're just part of a whole different mess."

"If you say so," she muttered. "And, of course, the bank ..." And she named the midsize one that she'd been talking about all along. "That's your final target."

A shocked silence came from the gunmen behind her, and she smiled again.

"You're bloody dangerous," the head guy replied in a thick heavy accent. "I don't know how the hell you even managed to figure that out."

"It was easy." She waved her hand in an airy motion. "People always think they can hide their tracks, but that's just not the way it is."

"Sure it is," he stated, "but what I don't know is how you got to that point."

"What difference does it make?" she asked. "You'll kill me anyway."

"You can bet that we'll kill you, but now I want to know how you got there."

"And I'm not telling you," she replied, with an exasperated tone.

"Oh, you'll tell us soon enough," he noted. "When we start shooting your little friend here, you'll start talking in no time at all."

The trouble was, they were right. She would. At that, Lachlan squeezed her fingers reassuringly. She wasn't so sure what was supposed to be so reassuring about the whole scenario because it just sucked. She hoped that Lachlan had some grand plan because she sure as hell had nothing.

When they reached a door at the end of this hallway, the head guy said, "Open the door, and no funny stuff."

Lachlan opened the door, which led to another series of

hallways.

"Now go forward."

And as soon as they got a little farther in, she heard the latch click shut. She turned in time to see the gunmen locking the door behind them.

The head guy turned and looked at her. "Yeah, you aren't going anywhere."

Shaky, she turned back again and looked over at Lachlan.

Then the guy added, "No talking."

Leah stared straight ahead. But she'd seen Lachlan wink at her.

And that, more than anything, reassured her, but it also worried her. Had the guys put together a plan and hadn't let her know? And, if so, why? And, if they had, what was the plan? She was confused, and she sure as hell would like something concrete to think about.

As they moved forward again, the head guy said, "Now stop."

She came to a stop, and Lachlan was told to open up the door on the left. He turned the knob, and they were led into a large room. At this point in time, she realized they would finally get to the truth of the matter because her boss was tied up and sitting here on the floor.

Ron took one look at her and started to cry.

She wasn't even sure what was going on. She turned to face her kidnappers and asked, "Why did you have to tie him up?"

"Because he's a watering pot," he replied, with a sneer.

At the same time, another door opened, and another man—whom she didn't recognize—stepped out. He was older, and, as she studied him, in the back of her mind was a vague memory of a picture she had glanced at. "Michael Danby," she said immediately.

He stared at her and gave a quick nod. "Yes, that's me. The joys of having a public service job."

"Yes. Not to mention the fact that you're connected to these idiots."

"No, I'm not," he stated. "Even if I am, it's not serious. I have nothing to do with this whole banking scheme."

"And that's because what you wanted was a whole lot different," she noted calmly.

He stared at her, looked at the two men, and dismissed them. "Stay outside and watch the entryway," he said. "I think I saw one of the other men out there earlier. One of her men," he clarified. "I don't trust any of them either. Before you go, knock this one out."

At that order, before she had a chance to react, Lachlan was hit from the side and dropped like a stone to the floor. She stared at him, tears welling in her eyes. "Why?" she asked quietly. "That's all he is to you?"

"That's all he is to anybody," Danby noted bitterly. "We live, and then we die."

"Unless we're stuck in between," she stated, with a knowing look in his direction.

At that, his gaze narrowed. "*Unless we're caught in between,*" he repeated, with a nod. "So you do know what this is all about?"

"I have a good idea," she replied. "The trouble is, I'm not exactly sure how involved you each are."

"We're not involved at all," he stated, with a shrug. "At least not in the way you're thinking."

"I know that you've got my boss tied up here and that you are his father-in-law and that his wife, your daughter, is bedridden with private nursing care."

"Sure," he agreed. "But are you aware that Ron deliberately ran over her with his vehicle? I had no way to prove it, of course. I gave it a really good try, but I couldn't get the prosecutor to take on the case," he stated bitterly. "My only child and this is what he does to her? He could have simply asked for a divorce, but no. ... He didn't want a divorce. That would be too simple. He wouldn't have gotten anywhere near as much money that way. No, ... no, he did it this way. If he'd killed her, at least she would be free, and he would have the insurance money, but he couldn't even do that right. He's such a fuckup. He didn't even have enough money to properly pay for her care. I had to pull in some favors to get him promoted to the point where he could cover the cost."

"I did what I could," Ron cried out.

"Sure you did, ... after you tried to kill her."

At that, her boss fell silent, the tears still running down his face.

She looked at him. "I already figured out that you had tried to kill her," she admitted quietly. "It breaks my heart to know you did that because, like Danby said, you could have just divorced her."

He stared at her in shock. "You already knew?" he asked, his voice rising painfully high.

She nodded. "Yeah, I figured as much, once I realized that people were helping you to cover your wife's medical costs."

"But all kinds of people would help cover medical costs," he stated in shock, as he stared at her.

"Sure, but then you also have a mistress."

He stared at her, the colors changing on his face as he

turned and looked at his father-in-law. "She's lying. … She's lying," he said to Danby. But to Leah, he replied, "He tried to get me killed."

She shrugged. "I'm not even sure what the penalty is for murder or for attempted murder at this point," she noted sadly. "Did you also kill Pamela?"

He stared at her in shock. "This isn't connected to that," he cried out. "Why would you even think that? I didn't do anything like that." He shook his head. "My God, how is everything so completely messed up?"

"So you had nothing to do with these bank-related murders or kidnappings or hostage-takings or the actual break-ins of or the hacks into the banks themselves?"

"No." Ron was sobbing loudly now, then looked up at her, as he realized something immediately, the shock registering on his face. "Why? Why would you even think that?"

"Because we tracked some of the money that came from one of the banks into your personal account. Then just as quickly transferred it to the Cayman Islands." He stared at her in horror, as she nodded. "I figured that somebody close to you probably set you up to take the fall."

At that, both Leah and her boss, Ron, turned their gazes toward Michael Danby.

Danby smiled at her. "You are good. Too bad you won't tell anybody about it."

"It is too bad, isn't it? Because, I mean, … it would at least have shown how clever you were. Of course not really clever enough because, well, I figured it out," she stated, "and that's when I realized you had the perfect lineup of influential people to help you."

"And who's that?" he asked, curious.

"An old school friend of yours," she replied. "Somebody who prefers to live in England."

"Not all the time," he argued.

"No, but that's his sticking point, isn't it? He goes over there, commits the crimes, and then chooses a place, like the south of Spain or something like that, where he lives for a while instead."

Danby shrugged. "He actually prefers Thailand now."

"Right, and you got him out of jail."

"No, I didn't," he corrected her. "He'd already served his time, so nobody gets to blame him for anything." Danby gave a laugh. "I didn't have anything to do with that. In fact, I didn't even reconnect with him until a few months ago. It took quite a while to set this up."

"Especially having it all point toward your son-in-law." She nodded. "I mean, if you couldn't get him to pay the price for the crime he committed, not only would this force us to look closer at his whole family scenario but you also made him suffer. If you could pin part of this bank scenario on him, he could still go down, if not for life then close enough, where he probably wouldn't survive prison anyway."

At that, Danby studied her with interest. "You know what? With a mind like that, you should go far."

"If I had a chance to go far, you mean."

"There is another slight problem that I need both of you for," Danby noted. "You see? Originally it would be enough to just have my own satisfaction on this *revenge on Ron* matter, but there was always the chance I wouldn't get away totally unscathed, so I had a backup plan."

"And backup plans, ... those are incredibly expensive."

He chuckled. "They're very costly, actually. You are correct."

"So, what's that got to do with me and Ron?" Leah asked.

"There was a connection to a certain bank in town."

She stared at him, then she turned and looked at Ron and asked, "What connection is that?"

Ron sighed. "My brother works at the midsize one," he admitted. "I thought you would have figured that out by now."

"I didn't really think about your brother as a viable suspect, considering you told me that he was deceased," she stated. "However, I was thinking about the fact that Pamela's family was involved with the board of that bank."

He stared at her. "Oh." He scrubbed at his face, then looked over at his father-in-law. "Did you kill her? She was so young," he cried out.

"I didn't kill her," Danby stated. "But, when you work with dangerous people, you have to feed them bits and pieces."

"And people like that are never satisfied," she added. "Your friend in England was busy taking advantage of the banks over there. You just wanted to steal from this one bank, and why is that?"

"Because they wouldn't fund her surgery," he replied, with a heavy voice.

"You realize that it was a lot of money, right?"

"Millions, but my daughter's care for the rest of her life would have also been in the millions. This treatment was something she couldn't do just once. It would have to be done over and over again. And that bank in particular, I have worked with and have helped considerably over the years. When they refused, I set out to destroy them. Making sure that, before I tore them apart, they understood why it was happening." He shook his head. "You never really understand people until you come up against a rock wall, and they turn and walk away from you."

"Somewhere along the line they must have decided that you were a bad bet," she noted.

"No, what they decided was that I was useless to them anymore. They'd been through a rough patch, and I had helped them get back on their feet, providing them with the right sources for guidance that they needed. I brought in experts to restructure everything, and, because of me, they are doing so well now." Danby laughed. "Suddenly they were fine. Yet then, when I needed help, they wouldn't give me the money," he snapped. "And this idiot here didn't even want to go to his brother's bank to begin with."

"It was a lost cause," Ron cried out. "Besides ..." Then he stopped, shaking his head. "What the hell. You know perfectly well that the treatment would just prolong her suffering."

"Yes, exactly. She was my daughter."

"You keep using past tense," Leah noted. "Why?"

Danby hesitated, then looked over at his son-in-law. "That's what triggered all this. She died a few weeks ago, just before the first one, ... when we were about to hit the first bank," he explained. "We postponed our plans, until we figured it out."

She turned and looked at her boss. "Seriously?"

"Yeah," he admitted. "I didn't tell anybody. I've been pretty rattled over the whole mess."

"Wow. So now she's dead, and you'll just what? Bury her, and hope nobody would ever know?"

"Yeah, that's what I was hoping for," Ron replied, "and then everything went to hell."

"But you couldn't stand to let that happen, could you?" She turned to Danby, with a grim expression.

"No way," Danby said. "That's when we made a few tweaks to the plan, to point to Ron as the guilty party. I wanted him to suffer for what he'd done to her, but, more than that, it was the thought of him going free after all this that made me sick to my stomach. And Ron's brother's bank? I was really hoping they would help us."

"So you made sure that they became part of your revenge plan too."

"And the other banks? Well, that was for my buddy," he noted, with a shrug. "Only afterward did I realize that I would need money myself, and we decided that this bank in particular would have to pay a bigger price, and that would be my ticket to freedom."

"So, why do I need to be here?"

He looked at her, then smiled. "Because we got through to Pamela and have a lot of codes for the target bank," he explained. "But Pamela somehow changed the codes and sent the new ones to you."

She stared at him in shock. "No, she didn't."

He nodded. "Yeah, she did. So you need to get them, and you need to get to work fast. I need those codes so we can wipe out the bank accounts that we are after," he added. "We're not after too many of them, just a few rather large ones," he said, with a wolfish smile. "And having to cover those losses will take down the bank, while giving me enough to live on. This guy? I'm afraid that instead of Ron having a chance to move on with his mistress for this new chapter of his life, he'll have a really bad accident."

At that, her boss cried out, "No, no, no. I won't. You don't have to do this anymore."

"No," Danby argued, "I do. I thought about letting you live and leaving you to stew in your guilt. However, once I realized you had a mistress, and you were planning on moving on without a thought of my daughter, I couldn't let that happen. You would just blab to everybody about a setup anyway, so I have to make sure you go down."

Danby spoke with such a cheerful tone in his voice that Leah knew he didn't care about Ron, and, in this case, Danby was quite happy to have Ron's part in this work out to Danby's advantage. "It is an interesting mess," she noted. "Did Pamela specifically tell you that she sent codes to me?"

He nodded. "Yeah, she did."

"You do realize that she probably lied, right?"

He stared at her. "No, I don't think so. She sent them to your old email."

She stared at him in surprise. "Seriously?"

He nodded. "You need to check."

"And if I don't?"

He pointed to Lachlan, who was still on the ground. "As a man who lost his only daughter, my only living relative, believe me when I say that I really don't care about any-body's life at this point. I'll take out whoever I need to take out. So, if you want him to live, I can just ignore him, while he's out cold. I mean, that's the easiest way for all concerned, but, if you want us to start blowing apart his kneecaps, that's okay too."

She took a deep breath. "Wow. You really are just a sorry son of a bitch, aren't you? Do you have a laptop?"

He smiled. "Of course I do. I'm so happy to hear that you'll be cooperative."

"And why should I be cooperative?" she muttered. "You'll just kill me anyway."

"You're smart too," he muttered. "I really like that about you." He turned and looked at his son-in-law with a deep and abiding hatred evident on his face. "Why the hell couldn't you have been like her?"

"I am like her," he cried out. "I'm her boss."

"No, you're not, and you're only her boss because I got you promoted," Danby snapped. "Otherwise you're just a dipshit, and the government wanted to get rid of you anyway, and the best way to get you out of their way, once I explained it to them, was to promote you. It happens all the time in big business," he noted. "Problems just get moved up on the escalator of success. It drove me nuts at the time, but I didn't know any other way to keep you under wraps and earning enough to pay for my daughter's care." He shook his head at him. "You are so pathetic. All you had to do was love her. That's all you had to do, but instead look what you did."

"I did love her," he cried out. "You know that."

"No, I don't," he replied sadly. "All I know is you're the asshole who tried to kill her, and actually, as far as I'm concerned, you did kill her. She died from the injuries you gave her, so you should go down for murder one."

"It wasn't premeditated," he said sadly. "We'd had a huge fight, and I just couldn't do it anymore. You know how she was. She had always been terribly unstable."

"She was unstable because of you," Danby snapped. "And, like I said, all you had to do was divorce her."

"You would never have accepted a divorce," he cried out. "That's not even something you would tolerate now with anybody. As far as you were concerned, she had to be happy at all times."

"And she should have been," he stated. "That was our

agreement. I only let you marry her because you were what she wanted. I thought she could have done much better, but oh no. … You convinced her that you were perfect. I agreed to it, but only under the caveat that you keep her happy."

"And I tried. I really … tried," Ron replied fervently.

"Yeah, I'm sure you did," Danby snorted. "Until you found someone else."

"We weren't very compatible. Nothing I did was right, but I tried."

"*Right.*"

It was obvious to Leah that Danby didn't care. As far as he was concerned, Ron had tried to murder his daughter, and that was it. And she had to admit that, if Ron had actually done it, well, … she had very little sympathy for him either.

But right now she was more concerned about herself and Lachlan. This whole story was fascinating and interesting and gave her a lot of answers to her questions. However, now that she was facing death, she realized how intriguing Lachlan was. How very different from the other men she knew, but this circumstance was looking as if her future could likely blow up in her face.

All she and Lachlan needed was some time together to see if something was really here between them. She wanted it to be so, but just because she wanted something didn't make it happen. And it sucked.

She opened up the laptop, and, under Danby's watchful eyes, she logged into an email account that she hadn't used much or in a while. "How would she have found this email?" she asked out loud.

"She chose to send the codes to that old email address, said that you'd set it up to have those emails forwarded to the new one for a while, but that had lapsed."

She nodded. "I did do that early on. I was working on several other projects and wanted to start with a clean slate. I almost never check this one."

As the emails loaded, she noted a few more than she expected. And, sure enough, there was one from Pamela. "Wow, look at that."

"It's there?" he asked eagerly.

"Yeah, it's here," she replied.

"Well, good. Log in so we can start transferring money into Ron's account."

She recognized the same Cayman Island routing info and numbering for their accounts. "Oh, look at that, the same account," she noted. "You might want to rethink that."

"Why is that?" he asked.

"Because it's the same account you used when you had the money earlier transferred from Ron's account."

"And that's perfect," Danby stated. "Because, once again, it'll all point back to him." And then he turned and glared at his son-in-law.

And it just might work, she thought, particularly if she wasn't around for the court case.

She quickly logged into the bank, using the information provided in the email. As soon as that was done, she set up the transfer. "You know that an amount like this will quite likely require approval."

"Nope, it won't," he stated. "I had Pamela set that up too."

"Jesus." And as soon as the money started to transfer over, she added details into her email.

"Now what are you doing?"

"Just answering the security questions," she noted.

"Pamela put it all into the email."

"Perfect," he replied.

As the connection worked away, she glanced down to see Lachlan staring at her. He was staying completely still, so clearly didn't want her to let on that he was awake. But his gaze was on her, and she could read the message in his eyes without too much trouble. She casually canceled the transfer.

"What are you doing?" Danby asked.

"The connection isn't going through," she stated, as she looked around. "I think it's probably the basement construction. We're just too deep for a good connection." He stared at her in frustration, until she raised her hands in frustration. "What do you want from me?" she asked. "I mean, look at it." As she pointed at the laptop screen, he could clearly see the words No Internet Connection.

He swore at that. Then he walked over to the door and called for the two henchmen. Both of them immediately stepped inside, and he told them, "We have to go to the surface. I want you to stay here with these guys."

The two gunmen nodded, then Danby grabbed her and said, "Bring the laptop. We're going outside." She grabbed the laptop, while Danby pocketed a handgun from one of the two men. "You guys keep this under control." He pointed her toward the hallway, asking where would be the best place for a good connection.

"There's a coffee shop on the ground floor. Or do you want to go to the main lobby?"

He stared at her for a moment. "I guess we can do it in the lobby, can't we?"

She nodded. "We should be able to. I mean, I haven't had any internet problems anywhere else in the building. But wherever we are now," she explained, "it's obviously too deep, and there's no connectivity."

He nodded. "Stupid modern times," he muttered under his breath. "We should have connectivity everywhere."

She stayed silent, and he pushed her out the door. She managed to get a quick look back at Lachlan. He winked at her, as she was propelled through the door.

THE MOMENT THE door slammed shut behind Leah, Lachlan was on his feet, and his right fist connected hard with the nearest gunman's jaw. That made a solid *crack*, even as the second man jumped on Lachlan's back. The first gunman hit the floor, and the gun left his hand, skidding toward Ron, who scrambled to pick it up with his hands tied.

Quickly flipping the second man off, Lachlan slammed him against the wall. He heard the *crack* of this gunman's body upon impact and then crunched him hard in the ribs, hearing another *crack* before dropping him too, giving him a right fist into the jaw for good measure. Lachlan walked over to Ron, snatched the gun from his still-tied hands. "Stay here."

And, with that, Lachlan raced out the door, leaving Ron still squawking behind him. Then Lachlan turned and headed down the hallway, hoping that he could catch up to Leah before Danby got her to the lobby. As soon as he came around a corner, he saw her up ahead. He immediately dashed up behind them, in case anybody saw him, as Danby pushed her toward the door.

Lachlan called out, "I'd stop right there if I were you."

At that, Danby turned slowly and looked at Lachlan. Both men held handguns. Lachlan didn't hesitate even for a moment and shot Danby, aiming for his gun hand. The bullet hit him in the wrist, sending the gun skittering off to the side.

Lachlan almost smiled as Danby cried out, holding his wrist against him and staring at Lachlan, in shock. As for Leah, she chased the gun down, picked it up, and immediately turned and held it on Danby too.

"Jesus Christ." Danby stared at the two of them. "How did you get free?"

"Because you forgot to secure me," he stated. "You had them knock me out, but my head is a whole lot stronger than that."

He stared at him in shock. "God, ... no, you can't stop it now." He shook his head in a panic. "We can't have that."

Lachlan got a closer look, seeing the blood dripping all over the floor. It was coming out way too fast. He pocketed the gun, then grabbed the man's tie from around his neck and wrapped it tightly around the wound. "He needs medical assistance," he told Leah. "Looks like I may have hit an artery."

She immediately stepped away and made some phone calls. Lachlan got Danby to sit on the floor and told him to hang on, but Danby just looked up at him, as if insane.

"No, it's better if I don't. Just let me die."

Lachlan shook his head. "No way, and here you are whining, when you had it all."

"No, when that asshole took down my daughter," he snapped, "I lost everything important."

Tears were in Danby's eyes, but Lachlan knew it wasn't for his wrist injury.

"So much loss," Danby said, "so much pain and all for nothing." Then he slumped to his side onto the ground.

Within minutes, the hallway exploded as people raced toward them.

Lachlan already knew it would be pretty hard to save Danby, but, if he got treatment quickly, there might be a chance to save his sorry life. As they stepped back, he grabbed Leah in his arms, removed the handgun from her fingers, and pulled her out of the way. "It's okay," he whispered, as he held her close.

She stared up at him, tears in her eyes, and whispered, "How is any of this ever okay?"

And he understood what she meant. As soon as they could—and he knew it would take some time, since they would have to provide statements—then he would take her away from here.

"Do you need to return to your office, or are you okay to head home?"

"I'd like to go home," she whispered, dropping her head to his chest. "I'd like a few days off, where I don't have to think about any of this." She lifted her head and stared at him. "But we need to catch everybody."

"That's not a problem," he replied. "I'll be busy for a couple days, making sure we've got all the parts and pieces of this one taken care of. By the way, we got a lead on the father and the daughter, and both seem to be shaken over their ordeal, but they are alive."

"Oh, that's wonderful to hear," Leah replied.

Lachlan nodded. "I thought you'd be happy to learn some good news. And I thought I'd stop by and see you when I got back."

She tilted her head up, then looked at him and smiled. "You'll have me to answer to if you don't."

At that, he grinned.

Markus stepped up. "Security will take her home," he told Lachlan. "We have to get going."

Lachlan looked down at her, and she whispered, "Come back, please."

He nodded, dropped a gentle kiss on her forehead, and disappeared.

CHAPTER 13

L EAH SAT IN her apartment.
It was three days later, and she hadn't heard from any of them in that time. She found it almost impossible to accomplish anything. She'd done what was needed for the various police and law enforcement agencies, plus her department at work, completing statements with as much detail as she could remember. That had been the hardest.

She'd been called up to her supervisors to give a full accounting, and what an accounting it was. As they all sat back and realized their vulnerabilities, they brought her in for verbal reports more than a few times. There were multiple headshakes as they tried to figure out how to handle all of the security holes, both physically and digitally, but that wasn't her problem. That would be other people's problem. She'd had enough on her own plate, just waiting and trying to figure out how she would handle it if Lachlan didn't return.

She refused to acknowledge that as a possibility because she knew that life just wouldn't be the same regardless. She'd found somebody who intrigued and delighted and infuriated her, all while making her smile at the same time, and surely that had to be worth a lot.

When her doorbell rang, she raced to the front door, then peered through the peephole. Gasping with delight, she opened the door, and, barely giving him time to enter her apartment, she threw her arms around his neck and hugged him close. He wrapped his arms around her and buried his face in the crook of her neck and held her.

They stood like that for a very long moment, and then she pulled her head back to take stock. "Are you okay?"

He dropped his forehead to rest against hers. "I am now."

"Did you handle everything?"

"Oh yeah," he replied, with a note of satisfaction.

She grinned. "And now what?"

"Now I have several days off, and then, apparently, I'm staying to learn some new computer skills."

She stared at him in growing delight. "Now that sounds great. And after that?"

"I don't know. I guess it depends on how things go. But I do have the option of transferring over here for a few months, at least until somebody else's transfer is completed." He raised an eyebrow. "And then we'll see."

She stared at him, as she realized what he meant. "Meaning, you might just stay here while I'm here?" she asked.

"Would that be a problem?"

"No," she whispered, "that would be awesome."

He chuckled. "How awesome?"

She threw her arms around his neck and kissed him passionately.

"That's a good start," he murmured, "but you might have to show me a little more appreciation than that."

"Oh, you think so, do you?" she teased, stepping back, with a cheeky grin. Then moved to the middle of the room and dropped the robe she'd been wearing, showing him absolutely everything there was to see. She watched him with a huge smile on her face, as he swallowed, his eyes bulging.

"God," he said, when he could get the words out. "You really do like to go from zero to sixty."

"I thought that you were a person who liked that too."

"Oh, God yeah." He was already tossing off his clothes, his hands hanging up on his belt.

She brushed away his hands and quickly took care of it, and, when his jeans dropped to the floor, she added, "Most people take off their shoes before their jeans."

"I'm a mess," he announced. "Somebody just showed me paradise and won't let me get there."

She burst out laughing. "Oh, you'll get there." She chuckled, as she bent down and helped him kick off his shoes. "You just need to slow down."

"No way am I slowing down." He suddenly was free, so he scooped her up into his arms and carried her to the bedroom, where he followed her onto the bed. As soon as his hot flesh landed on top of hers, she moaned and arched underneath him. "Wow." He gasped for control.

"Yeah, well, I've waited a long time. I'm not waiting anymore." And she wrapped her arms around him, and spreading her thighs, she wrapped her legs around his buttocks and lunged.

He shuddered in place. "Jesus, what happened to foreplay?"

"Yeah, that's for the next time," she whispered, enjoying his breath hot against her neck. "Unless of course you're not up to it?"

He rolled his eyes because the evidence was obvious between them, and, when he plunged deeper, she cried out in joy.

He hesitated and she murmured, "I'm fine. Don't you

dare stop."

At that, he started to move, his actions heavier, faster, and harder, until she exploded beneath him. And dimly, through her own waves of release, she heard him shout above her, before collapsing beside her. While he rolled over, she rolled with him, until she rested on his chest.

"Oh my God," he said, "you damn near killed me."

"Oh, I don't know about that. Looks like you rose to the occasion just fine."

He grinned at the innuendo. "This time," he admitted, "but I might need a moment."

"Yeah, you get a moment but not a moment extra." And, with that, she lowered her head and kissed him deeply, her tongue dueling with his. When she lifted her head again, she whispered, "Thank you for coming back."

"Are you kidding? I did everything I could to get here."

"And I believe you," she murmured. "I really do. I'm just grateful that now it's time for us."

"Hell, I wasn't even sure that I was on the right track with you."

"I know," she admitted. "It was really hard when I worried that I wouldn't see you again, possibly ever. Then I realized just how much I wanted to explore this and to see if we had a chance together."

"You and me both," he admitted gently. "And speaking of exploring ..." He shifted his hips and bounced her ever-so-lightly up and down a couple times.

She chuckled. "Yeah, we have a lot of exploring to do. And, as long as you're here for a few months, there is absolutely no rush."

"Says the woman who accosted me at the doorway," he noted, with a laugh.

She grinned. "I don't recall hearing any arguments against it."

"Hell no. I'm just waiting for you to stop talking so we can do it again."

She smiled. "In that case …" She lowered her head and started round two.

EPILOGUE

PAXTON FULLER STOOD in front of Mason. "Sir?" he asked hesitantly.

Mason looked up at him. "Yes?"

"I had asked for a transfer."

"Right," he replied, "and I have agreed to it, but I'm getting some flak from above."

He frowned at that. "Why?"

"I can't tell you that because frankly they don't always tell me these things. But maybe you've crossed somebody you shouldn't have."

"I don't think so," he replied cautiously.

"Good then. In that case, chances are the transfer will come through. It just might take a little longer than we hoped."

"Damn." He groaned and rotated his neck.

"Are you doing okay?"

"Yeah, I took a bit of a hit on the last mission," he replied, "so I am still doing physio."

"Are you cleared for work?"

"I thought I would be, but the physiotherapist wasn't terribly happy with my last session."

"In that case, that could be what the delay is," Mason noted. "Maybe you should head home and get some rest."

He nodded. "I was just on my way home when I saw

you in here. I know I shouldn't be bothering you, but you know when you want something really bad that you can almost taste it? I just figured maybe I'd ask."

"Maybe it's the paperwork."

He rolled his eyes at that. "In that case the transfer will never get done."

"Hey, paperwork snafus happen all the time. What's your marital status?"

"Not married, sir."

"Ever been married?"

"Nope, definitely not," he replied. "Our type of work is hard on a relationship."

"It is until you find the right person," Mason noted.

"I haven't been lucky enough to do that."

Mason looked at him and smiled. "You never know. I suggest you check to make sure that the paperwork is all clear and that there are no problems on that side."

"I can do that," he stated. "Is there anybody in particular I should talk to?"

"Yeah, her name is Sharees," he replied. "She should be in her office still." Mason checked the clock on the wall. "Yeah, she's there. Maybe run by on the way home."

"That sounds great," he said. "After all, it is what it is."

"And remember. The only way we keep doing what we're doing is by keeping healthy."

"Will do."

With that, Paxton headed down to the admin offices, and, as he walked in, there was a lineup. He waited off to the side, and, when it was his turn, he stepped up and said, "I'm supposed to speak with Sharees."

"I'm Sharees," replied the beautiful redhead in front of him, smiling. "What can I do for you?"

"Mason sent me," he murmured.

"Mason, *huh*? What kind of trouble are you in?"

"Nothing, I hope," he said. "I'm supposed to check to make sure there's no problem with the paperwork for my transfer request."

"Ah, he asked me about that. Just give me a minute." He watched as she headed to some paperwork on her desk. She picked up something, read it, and then walked back over. "Your physio isn't happy," she stated simply.

"I know, but it's not major."

"No, not major," she replied, with that smile again, "just major enough."

"Enough to hold it back?"

"Let's just say, until you clear the next session," she explained, "you're held back."

"Damn. Who was that? Was it Western?" She nodded, and he pulled out his phone. When it was answered, he said, "Hey, Western. It's Paxton Fuller."

"Yeah, what going on?"

"Did you really sideline me over that physio?"

"Yeah, I sure did." And then in the background came a different voice, followed by Western's horrified yell. "Hey! What are you doing?"

Confused, Paxton waited.

Rapid gunfire slammed through his phone connection. He stared at Sharees in shock.

"Oh my God! What was that?" she asked.

He hated the immediate thought that came to mind, but all he could think about was his physio would never sign off now.

He couldn't because, chances were, the man was dead. And when Paxton thought about everybody else in that office, he whispered to Sharees, "Call security."

"And say what?"

"Give them the address of my physio," he stated. "I'm on my way there." And, with that, he took off, hoping to find anyone alive. He could only hope he found Western before it was too late.

This concludes Book 28 of SEALs of Honor: Lachlan.

Read about Paxton: SEALs of Honor, Book 29

SEALS OF HONOR: PAXTON BOOK 29

Paxton, while trying to get clearance to return to work, calls his physio to ask why he's refusing to sign off on his documents—only to hear gunfire through the phone, killing the man he was talking too. Racing to the scene, he finds the gunman still there, in anguish and in fury, telling Paxton a tale of blackmail and fraud, before killing himself.

Hearing the same phone conversation that Paxton made while in her office, Cherise races behind to make sure he's okay, as the police move in. Standing together at the scene of the crime, however, puts them both in the target zone, as someone tries to keep the details of the blackmail a secret.

Trying to keep Cherise and himself safe, while unravelling the rot going on under the surface, Paxton realizes just how personal this case has become …

Find Book 29 here!

To find out more visit Dale Mayer's website.

http://smarturl.it/DMSLachlan

Author's Note

Thank you for reading Lachlan: SEALs of Honor, Book 28!
If you enjoyed the book, please take a moment and leave a
short review.

Dear reader,

I love to hear from readers, and you can contact me at my
website: www.dalemayer.com or at my Facebook author
page. To be informed of new releases and special offers, sign
up for my newsletter or follow me on BookBub. And if you
are interested in joining Dale Mayer's Reader Group, here is
the Facebook sign up page.
https://smarturl.it/DaleMayerFBGroup

Cheers,
Dale Mayer

COMPLIMENTARY DOWNLOAD

DOWNLOAD a **_complimentary_** copy of TUESDAY'S
CHILD? Just tell me where to send it!

http://dalemayer.com/starterlibrarytc/

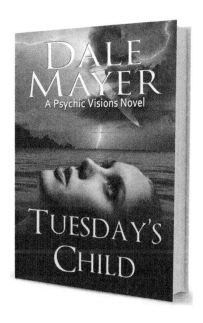

About the Author

Dale Mayer is a *USA Today* best-selling author, best known for her SEALs military romances, her Psychic Visions series, and her Lovely Lethal Garden cozy series. Her contemporary romances are raw and full of passion and emotion (Broken But … Mending, Hathaway House series). Her thrillers will keep you guessing (Kate Morgan, By Death series), and her romantic comedies will keep you giggling (*It's a Dog's Life*, a stand-alone novella; and the Broken Protocols series, starring Charming Marvin, the cat).

Dale honors the stories that come to her—and some of them are crazy, break all the rules and cross multiple genres!

To go with her fiction, she also writes nonfiction in many different fields, with books available on résumé writing, companion gardening, and the US mortgage system. All her books are available in print and ebook format.

Connect with Dale Mayer Online

Dale's Website – www.dalemayer.com
Twitter – @DaleMayer
Facebook – facebook.com/DaleMayer.author
BookBub – bookbub.com/authors/dale-mayer

Also by Dale Mayer

Published Adult Books:

Shadow Recon
Magnus, Book 1

Bullard's Battle
Ryland's Reach, Book 1
Cain's Cross, Book 2
Eton's Escape, Book 3
Garret's Gambit, Book 4
Kano's Keep, Book 5
Fallon's Flaw, Book 6
Quinn's Quest, Book 7
Bullard's Beauty, Book 8
Bullard's Best, Book 9
Bullard's Battle, Books 1–2
Bullard's Battle, Books 3–4
Bullard's Battle, Books 5–6
Bullard's Battle, Books 7–8

Terkel's Team
Damon's Deal, Book 1
Wade's War, Book 2
Gage's Goal, Book 3
Calum's Contact, Book 4

Kate Morgan
Simon Says… Hide, Book 1
Simon Says… Jump, Book 2
Simon Says… Ride, Book 3
Simon Says… Scream, Book 4
Simon Says… Run, Book 5

Hathaway House
Aaron, Book 1
Brock, Book 2
Cole, Book 3
Denton, Book 4
Elliot, Book 5
Finn, Book 6
Gregory, Book 7
Heath, Book 8
Iain, Book 9
Jaden, Book 10
Keith, Book 11
Lance, Book 12
Melissa, Book 13
Nash, Book 14
Owen, Book 15
Percy, Book 16
Hathaway House, Books 1–3
Hathaway House, Books 4–6
Hathaway House, Books 7–9

The K9 Files
Ethan, Book 1
Pierce, Book 2
Zane, Book 3

Lovely Lethal Gardens

Lifeless in the Lilies, Book 12
Murder in the Marigolds, Book 13
Nabbed in the Nasturtiums, Book 14
Offed in the Orchids, Book 15
Poison in the Pansies, Book 16
Quarry in the Quince, Book 17
Lovely Lethal Gardens, Books 1–2
Lovely Lethal Gardens, Books 3–4
Lovely Lethal Gardens, Books 5–6
Lovely Lethal Gardens, Books 7–8
Lovely Lethal Gardens, Books 9–10

Psychic Vision Series

Tuesday's Child
Hide 'n Go Seek
Maddy's Floor
Garden of Sorrow
Knock Knock...
Rare Find
Eyes to the Soul
Now You See Her
Shattered
Into the Abyss
Seeds of Malice
Eye of the Falcon
Itsy-Bitsy Spider
Unmasked
Deep Beneath
From the Ashes
Stroke of Death
Ice Maiden
Snap, Crackle...

What If…
Talking Bones
Psychic Visions Books 1–3
Psychic Visions Books 4–6
Psychic Visions Books 7–9

By Death Series
Touched by Death
Haunted by Death
Chilled by Death
By Death Books 1–3

Broken Protocols – Romantic Comedy Series
Cat's Meow
Cat's Pajamas
Cat's Cradle
Cat's Claus
Broken Protocols 1-4

Broken and… Mending
Skin
Scars
Scales (of Justice)
Broken but… Mending 1-3

Glory
Genesis
Tori
Celeste
Glory Trilogy

Biker Blues
Morgan: Biker Blues, Volume 1

Cash: Biker Blues, Volume 2

SEALs of Honor

Mason: SEALs of Honor, Book 1

Hawk: SEALs of Honor, Book 2

Dane: SEALs of Honor, Book 3

Swede: SEALs of Honor, Book 4

Shadow: SEALs of Honor, Book 5

Cooper: SEALs of Honor, Book 6

Markus: SEALs of Honor, Book 7

Evan: SEALs of Honor, Book 8

Mason's Wish: SEALs of Honor, Book 9

Chase: SEALs of Honor, Book 10

Brett: SEALs of Honor, Book 11

Devlin: SEALs of Honor, Book 12

Easton: SEALs of Honor, Book 13

Ryder: SEALs of Honor, Book 14

Macklin: SEALs of Honor, Book 15

Corey: SEALs of Honor, Book 16

Warrick: SEALs of Honor, Book 17

Tanner: SEALs of Honor, Book 18

Jackson: SEALs of Honor, Book 19

Kanen: SEALs of Honor, Book 20

Nelson: SEALs of Honor, Book 21

Taylor: SEALs of Honor, Book 22

Colton: SEALs of Honor, Book 23

Troy: SEALs of Honor, Book 24

Axel: SEALs of Honor, Book 25

Baylor: SEALs of Honor, Book 26

Hudson: SEALs of Honor, Book 27

Lachlan: SEALs of Honor, Book 28

Paxton: SEALs of Honor, Book 29

SEALs of Steel

The Mavericks

Ryker, Book 6
Miles, Book 7
Nico, Book 8
Keane, Book 9
Lennox, Book 10
Gavin, Book 11
Shane, Book 12
Diesel, Book 13
Jerricho, Book 14
Killian, Book 15
Hatch, Book 16
Corbin, Book 17
The Mavericks, Books 1–2
The Mavericks, Books 3–4
The Mavericks, Books 5–6
The Mavericks, Books 7–8
The Mavericks, Books 9–10
The Mavericks, Books 11–12

Collections
Dare to Be You…
Dare to Love…
Dare to be Strong…
RomanceX3

Standalone Novellas
It's a Dog's Life
Riana's Revenge
Second Chances

Published Young Adult Books:

Family Blood Ties Series
Vampire in Denial
Vampire in Distress
Vampire in Design
Vampire in Deceit
Vampire in Defiance
Vampire in Conflict
Vampire in Chaos
Vampire in Crisis
Vampire in Control
Vampire in Charge
Family Blood Ties Set 1–3
Family Blood Ties Set 1–5
Family Blood Ties Set 4–6
Family Blood Ties Set 7–9
Sian's Solution, A Family Blood Ties Series Prequel
    Novelette

Design series
Dangerous Designs
Deadly Designs
Darkest Designs
Design Series Trilogy

Standalone
In Cassie's Corner
Gem Stone (a Gemma Stone Mystery)
Time Thieves

Published Non-Fiction Books:

Career Essentials

Career Essentials: The Résumé

Career Essentials: The Cover Letter

Career Essentials: The Interview

Career Essentials: 3 in 1

Printed in Great Britain
by Amazon

79461636R00139